"There's a place on Third Street in Austin that has the best craft pizza... the best in the state," she said, unable to contain the excitement in her voice.

"That's where I took you on our first date, then," he said with a glimmer in his eyes that caused her stomach to free-fall.

"It was a perfect night," she said, continuing on with the cover.

"I knew the minute you ordered the special that there was something different about you," he said. His eyes lit up. His expression softened. The way he spoke about their fake date, almost like it was real, was incredibly sexy. "I never believed in love at first sight, but I sensed you were going to be important in my life."

Well, now she really was transfixed.

"The same was true for me," she said. "There was something about sharing that first slice that made my whole future flash before my eyes. Us. Kids. A house."

Quint cleared his throat, as if it had suddenly dried up.

UNDERCOVER COUPLE

USA TODAY Bestselling Author
BARB HAN

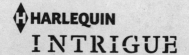

HARLEQUIN
INTRIGUE

All my love to Brandon, Jacob and Tori,
the three great loves of my life.

To Babe, my hero, for being my best friend,
my greatest love and my place to call home.

I love you all with everything that I am.

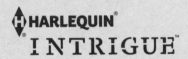

Recycling programs
for this product may
not exist in your area.

ISBN-13: 978-1-335-48956-2

Undercover Couple

Copyright © 2022 by Barb Han

Harlequin Enterprises ULC
22 Adelaide St. West, 41st Floor
Toronto, Ontario M5H 4E3, Canada
www.Harlequin.com

Printed in U.S.A.

USA TODAY bestselling author **Barb Han** lives in north Texas with her very own hero-worthy husband, three beautiful children, a spunky golden retriever/standard poodle mix and too many books in her to-read pile. In her downtime, she plays video games and spends much of her time on or around a basketball court. She loves interacting with readers and is grateful for their support. You can reach her at barbhan.com.

Books by Barb Han

Harlequin Intrigue

A Ree and Quint Novel

Undercover Couple

An O'Connor Family Mystery

Texas Kidnapping
Texas Target
Texas Law
Texas Baby Conspiracy
Texas Stalker
Texas Abduction

Rushing Creek Crime Spree

Cornered at Christmas
Ransom at Christmas
Ambushed at Christmas
What She Did
What She Knew
What She Saw

Decoding a Criminal

Visit the Author Profile page at Harlequin.com.

CAST OF CHARACTERS

Emmaline Ree Sheppard, aka Ree—This Alcohol, Tobacco and Firearms agent can't afford to fall for her partner, especially when he seems hell-bent on self-destruction.

Quinton Casey, aka Quint—This hotshot ATF agent blames himself for his pregnant partner Tessa's death and will stop at nothing to put the person responsible behind bars. Will he go too far?

Charley Davies—Is this restaurant owner running guns out of the back of his operation?

Bald Guy—He is hanging around the Greenlight Bar and Restaurant a whole lot and he seems shady.

Willie—He is the boyfriend of one of the waitresses and an all-around jerk, but is he involved in more than petty crime?

Dumitru—The ultimate target and person responsible for Tessa's murder is elusive—too much so?

Chapter One

Emmaline Ree Sheppard, aka Ree, squinted into the blaring south central Texas sun on what was turning out to be another scorching hot July morning. A wooden sign on the side of the road read Welcome to Cricket Creek, Home of the Annual Cricket Toss Festival. Ree involuntarily shivered as she connected a call with her brother. She would have to take a pass on that festival.

"Hey. What's up?" Shane asked.

"I pulled a marriage assignment. Newlyweds. I couldn't call you before now. Got any last-minute advice about what questions I need to ask my 'spouse' when I arrive? I won't have much time with him and you know I can't explain why," Ree said. Shane had been married the longest and she figured he would be the best go-to person in this situation. Pulling an assignment to work with a legendary agent like Quinton Casey strung her nerves tight and she wanted to be as ready as possible.

"How much time do you have before you get

to your assignment? Can you tell me that?" Shane asked.

"According to GPS—" she checked the screen "—less than five minutes."

"Wait...what?" Shane's surprise was laced with a familiar sound. All four of her brothers had warned her of the dangers of following in their father's footsteps, and that worry came across in their tone at times. Her mother still hadn't forgiven Ree for her career choice. At least Shane had been the only brother who hadn't tried to talk her out of working for a government agency in law enforcement. Still, his concern slipped in despite his attempt to cover with a cough.

"No time to explain and you know I wouldn't be at liberty to discuss a case anyway." She lifted her hand to shield her eyes from the now-blinding sun. "I have some ideas but need to know if I'm on the right track. What basics would a wife know about her husband?"

Shane took in a deep breath. "Okay, here goes. Off the top of my head, you should probably know favorite food, color, and what kind of drink he'd order at the bar."

"Right." Ree made a mental note. The drink question was golden as she would be interviewing for a waitressing job and her "husband" was likely to come in since they'd be living across the parking lot from the establishment. She gripped the steering wheel a little tighter as another minute ticked by. Four left. "What else?"

"Know the basics about his family, like how many brothers and sisters he has and what their names are. If he has parents, grandparents and whether they are living," Shane continued, his voice hitching on the last word. He often joked they all stuffed their feelings down like any good Irish Catholic family. They never talked about their father.

Another minute passed, reminding Ree she didn't have a second to spare.

"Got it." The little things could trip up an undercover operation, especially since she'd be flying straight out of the gate. She'd just completed her second year as an undercover agent for Alcohol, Tobacco and Firearms. This was her first "married" assignment. "Anything else?"

"I'm sure you'll discuss basics with your partner." Shane was right and she already knew pretty much everything he'd just said. Hearing her brother's voice calmed her nerves.

"He's a big deal in the department, from what I hear," she admitted.

"Then go in knowing your ground rules," Shane stated.

GPS let her know the location was coming up on her right. Two minutes had gone by in a blur.

"Got it," she said before pausing. "Thanks for the tips."

Ree stopped her sedan in front of the one-room cabin with a motorcycle parked in front. She hesitated, unable to bring herself to end the call.

"Even if he outranks you, don't let him intimidate you," Shane insisted.

"I grew up with four brothers," Ree said. "Since when have I ever let that happen?"

Shane laughed and the sound brought her nerves down a notch. She'd debated making the call but was glad she had. Her brothers could be overprotective at times. The word *overbearing* came to mind. She'd worked her whole life to prove she could stick up for herself. And yet, at times like these, she still needed her family.

"Valid point," Shane conceded.

"I hear this agent can be a real hothead," she said.

"Since when have you not been?" Shane teased, echoing her words. "Mom accuses your temper of coming from the Irish side of the family."

"I have the red hair to prove the Irish part," she quipped, thinking it had been too long since she'd seen her family.

"Speaking of Irish, Preston asked about you the other day," Shane said.

"And you're bringing this up to me right now?" she asked, not bothering to hide her frustration. Preston had been the closest she'd come to going all in with a boyfriend. He also happened to be her older brother's best friend.

"Right. Bad form. Forget I even said anything," Shane said along with an apology.

"Already done." She did her best to keep the hurt out of her voice at the memory of her ex. Preston was the only one she'd second-guessed walking away from. She had her reasons for ending the fling. But then, her brother pointed out she had her running shoes parked at the door every time she started to get serious in a relationship. Whether he was right or wrong, Ree had realized she needed to draw the line at having her brothers involved in her romantic life.

"Hey, sis. Be careful," Shane warned as she heard her three-year-old nephew Liam wail in the background.

"You know it." She pulled in beside the Ducati Diavel motorcycle, about to meet her "husband" for the next few days, possibly weeks. "Kiss Liam for me."

"Come home and kiss him for yourself," Shane quipped and then seemed to realize she didn't stay away so much because of her nephew. "Or you could FaceTime."

"I can take a day off when this assignment is over. I'll be sure to stop by or call him then," she promised. "Give Evelyn a hug for me and kiss baby Cara in the meantime."

"Will do. And I'll hold you to the visit," Shane said as Liam's howling got even louder.

"I knew you would," she said before bidding goodbye and ending the call.

Ree had no idea when that might be. The assignment to see if the bar owner was involved in arms dealing was on its own timeline. Working with a reputed agent—one she was about to meet for the first time—when she'd just celebrated her second year on the job after a promotion had her nerves on edge. She could do this, she reminded herself.

Shane's advice to go in strong was probably right. Someone with Quinton Casey's background would want a confident partner.

A couple of deep breaths for fortitude and Ree cut off the engine before grabbing her purse. The hot late-morning air slammed into her as she stepped out of the junkpile she'd been issued for the assignment. The run-down teal green Ford Fiesta's door groaned as she banged it shut.

A wall of humidity hit with the force of a rogue wave and had a similar impact as she stood in the sweltering heat. She plucked at her white button-down blouse, regretting the high but fashionable collar, trying not to soak herself with sweat before she met the man inside the cabin. Her high-waisted forest green pants fit well enough to show off long legs that she'd worked hard to tone at the gym. The cuffs struck just above her ankles. Her auburn hair was styled in a low side pony. Black, spiked heels rounded out the interview outfit.

As she balled her hand into a fist and then raised it to knock, a wave of panic gripped her and a knot formed in her stomach. There was no other way to get through this first meeting than face it head-on. Agent Quinton Casey had a reputation for coming on like a bull. She steadied herself, getting ready for the charge that was sure to come at her.

Besides, stand in the sun any longer and she might actually melt. Before she lost her nerve, she knocked. Of course, then she realized she should have used the key. It was a simple mistake. Anyone could have made it. And yet, humiliation burned at the misstep. This assignment wasn't off to a good start and she prayed it wasn't a bad omen.

"Door's open," came the masculine voice—a voice that was like whiskey over ice.

She opened it and stepped inside, immediately shutting the door behind her.

Agent Casey practically sneered at her as she stared at the hulk of a man standing on the other side of the one-room cabin. His muscled torso formed an improbable V at the waist, and even with day-old stubble on his chin the man would be considered hot by most standards. Seeing him in person, she wished someone had prepared her for his sheer size. He had to be six feet three inches, with the kind of body most athletic recruiters would kill for if he was college age. It wouldn't surprise her at all to learn he'd played ball in his youth. He had the whole "chiseled jawline, strong, hawklike nose and piercing eyes" bit down pat. Her pulse kicked up a few notches just looking at the man. She couldn't afford to be distracted or intimidated.

Her brother's voice rang in her head. *Go in knowing your ground rules.*

The famous Agent Casey stood there like he was issuing a challenge, as expected. She'd heard the rumors he'd become difficult to work with, and knew she would get one shot to make a first impression. She needed to be strong. More of her brother's words came to mind. *Don't let him intimidate you.*

Summoning all her courage, she started right in. "Okay, so this is how it's going to go."

"Do tell," he said, his voice a study in calm but his gaze practically boring a hole through her.

She could admit her nerves had her coming on a little stronger than intended. Taking another deep breath, she resolved to soften her tone.

"We don't have long before I have to be next door for my interview," she said. "So, just to make sure we're on the same page, my favorite color is blue, and my second favorite color is green. Now you go."

He didn't respond or seem amused. Instead, he gripped the counter's edge until his knuckles turned white.

Her bravado faltered. She checked her watch, needing to head next door sooner than she'd like. She didn't want to be late to her interview and she needed to have a few basics down to sell the lie in case the conversation turned casual and her future employer asked questions about her spouse.

"Green like a garden hose or like a leprechaun?" he finally asked, crossing his feet at the ankles and then folding his arms across his chest. There was a slight smirk on his face as he leaned his hip against the counter.

"We don't have a whole lot of time to lay the groundwork before I have to head next door and land a job, or this assignment is over before it started. So maybe you want to take this a little more seriously?" She tapped the toe of her shoe on the dated wood flooring. The man was being annoying. He wasn't the only one who could fold his arms over his chest. She mimicked his stance and that seemed to further amuse him.

No response came. His eyes belied his casual demeanor. Even from across the room she could see a storm brewed in those sapphire blues.

"What's your favorite beer?" she asked, refusing to be intimidated. If he was testing her, she intended to pass with flying colors. In fact, she excelled at taking tests. So this guy needed more than a smirk to throw her off.

Not only did he not respond, but he yawned. Okay, he must be trying to get under her skin. See how far he could push? Test her? She needed to regroup. Come at this from a different angle.

"Fine. Let me tell you my ground rules before this whole—" she waved her arms in the air "—newlywed thing gets started."

He dropped his head. His boot suddenly became real interesting to him. This way, she couldn't read his reactions and she had no idea if this was part of the test or not. His first move was to throw her off her game. His point there. She definitely felt on edge. His reputation had her playing defense when she should be playing offense. She was starting to second-guess herself and to wonder whether or not she was the right person for this assignment.

Nerves were good, she reminded herself. Being afraid would keep her mind sharp. She'd been on several dozen undercover assignments so far. This one would be no different. Of course, she would have a few more nerves working with Agent Casey. This assignment was serious, a possible career maker. The agency wouldn't partner her with the A-team if this was a no-brainer.

There was no reason to be unnerved by Agent Casey despite how quickly her pulse climbed with him in the room. He was a man just like every other, despite being disquietingly good-looking. He might be a few steps ahead of her professionally, but she was a quick study.

Some of her bravado was shrinking but she wasn't going to let that stop her. Shane was right. Go in strong. *Be brave.*

Ree cleared her throat and continued, "Holding hands is fine, so is incidental touching. In fact, the more the better because we're supposed to be newlyweds." All she could remember from her brother's first year of marriage was how lovey-dovey he and his new wife, Evelyn, had been. The thought of physical contact with Casey caused her stomach to free-fall. "So feel free to touch me but watch it. I don't want to have to file any conduct reports when this is all done."

Casey didn't immediately speak. The longer the silence stretched on, the higher her nerves climbed, until they were strung so tight she thought they might snap.

When she was just about to tell him he needed to start cooperating, he looked up at her. Those intensely blue eyes of his locked onto her as he closed the distance between them in a few quick strides. Despite her heart galloping and all her warning signals flaring, she stood rooted to the spot, strangely transfixed. By this point, her heart was beating wildly in her chest and her instincts said *run*. But she didn't get to be *who* she was or *where* she was by giving in to fear, so she challenged him with her gaze, daring him to keep going. That worked right up until he took the final threatening step toward her that had her automatically stepping back until the wall trapped her.

He brought his hands up to cup her cheeks, tilting her face toward his. And then he brought his lips down on hers, hard and unyielding. All Ree could do was surrender to the heat flowing inside her, and the pressure building. There was so much passion and promise in the kiss that her brain was swimming in a fog. She couldn't remember the last time she'd been so thoroughly swept off her feet, but his lips moving against hers were pure heaven.

They were gone almost as quickly, leaving cold air between his face and hers. She slowly opened her eyes to meet the most intense stare she'd encountered in her life. Her breath caught and she had to swallow to ease the sudden dryness in her mouth.

"Let me tell you my rules," he practically ground out. "Nothing is more important than catching the bad guy. So, if that means kissing on the lips, so be it. You don't have to enjoy it and neither do I, but be clear on this one point—my only responsibility is to make sure a slimeball ends up behind bars when this is all said and done."

Ree met his gaze head-on and with bravado she didn't feel said, "Fine. Can we get to work now?"

"Fine," he parroted, obviously a little thrown off she hadn't crumbled or ripped into him. "Where would you like to start?"

"Names," she said. "What do we call each other in public?"

"It's probably easier if we stick to our actual first names, so I went ahead and had documents made up. You can call me Quint or *honey*," he said before retrieving a pair of wedding bands. He handed one over to her and then slipped the other on his finger. "Just please don't call me *babe*. It's fingernails on a chalkboard."

"Got it," she said, figuring there was a story there somewhere. "I'm Ree. And ditto on the *babe*. Not my cup of tea, either. What's our last name?"

"Matthews," he supplied before walking over to a duffel bag and taking a knee. A couple of seconds later, he produced a wallet. "There are credit cards in there and a DL in your new identity."

Ree took the offering, ignoring the frisson of electricity when their fingers grazed. She traded out her wallet and handed the old one over to be locked in the tackle box he retrieved next. "The job next door was advertised so I'm guessing that means the owner—"

She stopped midsentence, reaching for the name.

"Charley Davies," Casey… *Quint* supplied.

She nodded and flashed a smile. "Right. I need to remember that, considering I'll be meeting with him soon."

"His name is on the ad, so that's a good idea," he agreed. Then he added, "My story is that I was part owner in a moving company and had a career-ending accident." He pointed to a boot. "We're moving here to save money while I go to online school for computer programming certification."

The timer dinged on her phone. She glanced over at Quint and nodded. "Time to go meet Mr. Davies."

QUINT DIDN'T EXPECT to feel the stab of guilt at hurting Ree's feelings earlier. She'd bucked up and held her ground, but a split second of hurt had darkened her eyes, and he'd felt two inches tall. Both were skilled at covering their emotions. He'd read her jacket. She was a solid agent with an impressive track record.

He cursed himself again for the way he'd treated her. She'd come on too strong and he'd reacted. His reaction caught him off guard. He had half a mind to text his boss and tell her what a bad idea it was to force him to work with a partner, *any* partner. Quint did his best work alone. But he'd convinced a psychiatrist and his boss that he didn't have any hangups after Tessa's death. If he went back now and said he couldn't work with another female partner they'd know he was struggling. He'd gone to great lengths to stay on the job because that was his only tether to sanity. Besides, what would he tell his boss? Life was hard? Quint hadn't gotten over the past?

Nope. There was only living with it and trying to get through this case so he could move on to the next, then a few more until he got his rhythm back. Stay on the horse another day and then another, until saddling up felt like the most normal thing again.

The sexual current running between him and Ree had unnerved him. The kiss had been meant to prove a point. It wasn't supposed to rattle Quint like it had. It was the only reason he could be affected by Ree. No big deal. He would get over it and get on with his job.

Quint started pacing in the one-room cabin. The place had everything the two of them needed to survive this case: a kitchenette, a bathroom, a living room and bedroom combined. The hall closet held a stackable washer and dryer. Definitely a bonus. The sofa was a pullout. He could sleep on the lounger and give her the bed over to one corner. It was the least he could do after being a jerk.

Ree had been something to look at in her blouse, pants and heels. The white fabric had hugged ample breasts. The green of her pants highlighted her eyes—eyes that were shielded by the thickest, blackest lashes he'd ever seen. The way those eyes had sparkled with something that looked a helluva lot like need when he'd kissed her had sent his pulse skyrocketing.

He chided himself on the bad form. Those green eyes, her stubborn chin, had thrown him completely off his game when she'd challenged him. At least he'd pulled it together. The conversation had gotten back on track. A very large part of him wanted to march next door so he could spy on what was going down. The setup was that Ree was supposed to be trying to get a job as a waitress. When she got on the inside, he would come over as her husband, a guy who was trying to better his life by going back to online school for computer programming.

Once they established a relationship with the owner, Quint would "volunteer" to help with computer needs either as a thank-you for hiring his wife or a thank-you for the occasional free lunch. Quint would have to feel Charley Davies out to see which tactic would work best.

He stabbed his fingers through his hair, wishing he was the one next door selling their cover. This was the hardest part of working with a new partner.

Ree was a professional; she could do this. If not, he would figure out a way to salvage their cover story and infiltrate the establishment that was part bar and part restaurant for foodies.

Ideally, Quint and Ree would have had more time together before she had to go in. An icy chill ran down his back at the thought something might happen to her. No, Quint. This was Ree, not Tessa.

He managed to keep at bay the flashbacks of his former partner's fatal injury while on an assignment together, practically wearing a hole in the wood floor from pacing in a circle, wishing the hell that the door would open and Ree would come back with a job secured.

The clock said she'd only been gone twenty minutes, but it felt like an eternity. Going next door might make him seem too eager. It might raise a few red flags. Quint issued a sharp sigh.

A half hour later, with still no sign of Ree, he decided he couldn't afford to sit around and wait for her to return. Charley Davies might have seen right through her. She might have given herself away. She could be locked in a closet, or worse. A half dozen scenarios ran through his mind, none of them good. More flashbacks stamped his thoughts. Tessa in the hospital. The beeping sound of the machine temporarily keeping her alive. The utter and complete silence when the doctor flipped the switch to off. Anger shot through Quint. White-hot fury boiled inside his veins. He couldn't afford to spiral down that dark, familiar path.

There was no way he could stay here without knowing if his new partner was in trouble.

Chapter Two

The best way to disarm someone was to gain their sympathy. Part of Quint's cover involved wearing a walking boot that made it seem like he was recovering from an injury. His physical size could put the bar owner on the defensive, so the boot was meant to convey weakness and vulnerability. He slid his left foot inside and pulled the straps tight. Then he double-checked his ankle holster where his SIG Sauer was secured. Everything was good to go there.

Quint made the trek next door to the combo restaurant and bar. Dark images edged into his thoughts. He stopped them right there, gave himself a mental slap and shook his fear off. Getting inside his head would be bad for him and his partner. Let the past creep up, and he might as well hand over their cover. He needed to keep his head in the game.

He and Ree needed to go over the list of employees when he got her home. There was still a whole lot to discuss.

Surveying the lot, he took note of six cars, three trucks, four motorcycles and three parked RVs. He

skimmed the license plates as he walked past, memorizing as many as he could and observing that several were from out of state. This wasn't the time to
rebuke himself for not thinking to capture a few of
the license plates with his cell phone while he was
still inside the cabin a few moments ago.

There was very little in the way of surveillance
equipment in the parking lot. Small towns were
known for being safe and for residents having each
other's backs. An illegal operation could have mul-
tiple people involved, including the county sheriff.
Ree hadn't been brought up to speed on the fact the
bar owner and sheriff were second cousins. Even if
they weren't in league, the bar owner would know
the sheriff's blind spots. Family could be a huge
blind spot. The single mother who'd raised him was
nothing short of an angel in his eyes. After some of
his stunts, she probably deserved sainthood. And
he would do anything for her if she was still alive.
Families usually could be counted on to cover for
each other.

As Quint reached for the door handle, a big, burly
biker-looking guy with one of those handlebar mus-
taches pushed it open from the inside and took a
couple of steps before holding it for Quint. "Here
you go, man."

He wore black from head to toe and sported a
leather vest with the Harley Davidson logo on the
left-hand side. At least his T-shirt was short-sleeved
in this heat. Quint assumed the man owned one of
the motorcycles in the parking lot.

"Appreciate it," Quint said with a nod.

Once inside, he immediately skimmed the restaurant, taking it all in. His gaze stopped at the bar area on the left-hand side of the room, back corner. The darkened bar wasn't open for the lunch crowd. Otherwise the place was brightly lit, with open seating, cafeteria style. There were at least a dozen tables scattered around the main section.

In the center of the back wall, there was a pair of stainless steel doors leading into what must be the kitchen. They had twin windows that looked more like portals on a cruise ship. One of the doors was marked In, and the other, Out.

The restaurant buzzed with conversation. It had a little bit of a retro diner feel to it, with glossy, red vinyl booths lining the perimeter. The tables were small four-tops with stainless steel chairs that had cushions in the same material as the booths. The setup was reminiscent of a 1950s soda fountain, and the smells coming out of the kitchen made his mouth water. This was the kind of place that he could easily see ending up on one of those diners-and-dives shows on TV. There was original art hanging on the walls with handwritten price tags. Locals?

Quint's blood pressure started to climb when he didn't immediately see Ree. If he was the owner and the restaurant was this busy, he would park someone he was interviewing in the bar area. The fact she wasn't there or anywhere else in view kicked up his racing pulse a few more notches.

He studied the faces of the people at the tables.

They were some families, some locals as well as foodie types on the road who were making a pit stop on their way somewhere else. Then there was the biker club. Several sat in a corner booth, hunkered over their plates and barely mumbling a word to each other as they ate. He would keep an eye on them.

The restroom sign to the right caught his eye. He took a couple of steps toward it and saw a long hallway. There was a counter and stools over there. Looked like the place had counter service for single diners.

A college-age waitress in a blouse that was unbuttoned down practically to her belly button and tied off underneath her breasts bounded toward him. She had on leather bike shorts and white boots.

"Just one today?" She smiled at him. Her cheeriness seemed forced and her cheeks flushed as she picked up a menu.

"That's right," he confirmed.

"Booth, counter or table?" She practically beamed at him, her gaze sliding down his body, stopping at his boot. He could have sworn she frowned.

"Counter." He figured that area would afford the best visuals to the kitchen. The spot would block most of his view of the restaurant and he wouldn't see any of the bar area, but a sacrifice had to be made.

Quint needed to know where Ree was, and he needed to know now.

"Right this way." The waitress's name tag read Zoey.

Quint focused on the tile floor and its black-and-white checkered pattern as he followed Zoey to his stool. The area looked straight into the kitchen. The waitress stopped and faced the kitchen, leaving very little room between her and the stool. Rather than risk touching her, he walked around to the other side instead. Was flirting part of the job? She looked young enough to be his daughter, so the move did little more than cause his stomach to churn.

A frown brought the corners of her mouth down and creased her forehead. It was more than a frown... a pout? Even if Quint wasn't "married" on this assignment, Zoey was far too young for his liking. When he dated, he went for someone closer to his age, someone who liked the same era of music and was more than a pretty face. He liked someone he could have a real conversation with. Someone who set her phone down when she spoke to him. Call him low-tech, but he preferred to talk to someone who looked at him during a conversation and not at a screen. Then again, flirting might be part of the job.

Zoey made a humph noise before asking, "Can I get you anything to drink?"

"Coffee and water," he stated as he scanned the kitchen staff.

His gaze stopped on Ree. She stood at the order counter across from the kitchen staff, balancing a tray in one hand while taking plates off the counter with the other. Her coordination skills were on point: he'd give her that. Relief washed over him that she wasn't tied up somewhere, bound and gagged.

She wore the same outfit as Zoey. The shirt showed

off way too much of her ample cleavage and those shorts hugged her body like…

Never mind. Suffice it to say the company uniform didn't get two thumbs-up from her "husband."

As she turned, their eyes caught, and a look of panic crossed her features. Quint cleared his throat and looked down at the menu, figuring he'd caught her off guard and thrown her out of her comfort zone.

Again, he kicked himself.

If he could read her, then so could a seasoned criminal. There was no way Quint could protect her without being by her side 24/7. Now that she'd met the owner, maybe they could come up with an excuse for her to disappear. Something sudden could have happened in the family, like her mother falling ill. It would be for Ree's own good.

Quint stopped himself right there, the dark hole threatening to drag him under. He put his face in his hands and then rubbed the scruff on his chin. This assignment was nothing like the one that had killed Tessa.

"WHAT ARE YOU doing here?" Ree forced a smile as her new coworker joined them, bringing coffee and water to Quint. Her gaze dropped to his lips—lips she'd been trying to forget since leaving the cabin more than an hour ago.

"Came to look at my beautiful wife," he said, shooting her a look that threatened to melt all her carefully constructed defenses. This man was good. A little too good if anyone asked her.

"I'm working right now, honey," she said as her cheeks flushed. A look passed behind those serious blue eyes of his. She'd scored a direct hit on something. No idea what it meant, though. She made a mental note to figure it out later when they were alone. The thought of being holed up in a one-room cabin with a man who caused her pulse to skyrocket every time she looked at him didn't do good things to her blood pressure.

Ree took in a deep breath. Rather than panic, she could use her nerves to her advantage. They made her bold. She set her tray down, leaned over the counter and drew on her most seductive smile. "But I'll see you at home later."

Quint's gaze momentarily dipped and her cheeks warmed. She realized the move had given him a bird's-eye view of her cleavage.

He cleared his throat like he couldn't find his voice.

"Is that a promise?" His voice was a low, throaty growl.

Ree smirked. She couldn't help it. Throwing Quint off his game even for a second was satisfying. Besides, the whole exchange would only sell the fact they were newlyweds.

Zoey took the hint, dropping off the drinks without so much as a word and beating feet so fast it looked like she was training for a track meet.

The sapphire color of Quint's eyes darkened with something that looked a whole lot like need when he locked gazes with Ree. She shouldn't gloat but, damn, it felt good to know she wasn't the only one who'd been affected by that kiss. Seemed like it might have been a two-way street and the ever-cool, ever-in-charge, living legend Quinton Casey had a moment, too.

"I gotta serve my customers." Ree picked up the tray and walked away, sashaying her hips.

Her ego had her taking a look back a moment before she walked away. Big mistake. Head down, Quint was studying his cup of coffee like it was a midterm and he was one failing grade away from being booted out of school.

After delivering food to her table, she didn't get much chance to look at Quint again considering the next hour was nonstop. The restaurant was bustling, which was good for tips and a great way to prove herself to Charley Davies. Her interview with the man had lasted all of three minutes when he'd gone to a locker in the backroom, tossed her a uniform—if it could be called that—and then asked if she could start immediately. Business was picking up.

She'd nodded, smiled and gone into the restroom to try on the getup. It fit. Charley had a good eye for sizing, but she also figured he only hired one size, and could easily be classified as a chauvinist. The way he'd eyed her up and down when they'd first met had her wanting to take a shower. He'd stopped short of apologizing when he casually mentioned his customers were picky about who served them.

Letting the comment go went against her nature. Her brothers might pick on her but they never treated her like she was breakable or couldn't handle their teasing. In many ways, she was just like one of them and they were equal opportunity pranksters. Stuffing down her feelings wouldn't be easy, but this was her job and she reminded herself of the greater good she was doing.

Besides, her immediate reaction to Charley was that he was guilty of something. It was her job to figure out what it was, because last she checked, being a restaurant/bar owner who only hired a certain type wasn't technically against the law.

Three hours after her interview, the lunch crowd waned. At some point, Quint had gone home. And the waitresses were down to filling ketchup bottles to prep for the dinner crowd that—she checked her watch—would start in roughly an hour. All she wanted to do was go home and put her feet up. Being on the go for literally three hours straight without so much as a restroom break took a toll. Her dogs were barking.

"Great job today." Charley's voice right behind her caught her off guard.

She gasped, and then spun around.

"Thanks," she managed to say.

"Looks like you'll be a good addition to the family," he said. Charley was tall, with a runner's build. He had sandy blond hair and gray eyes. Some might consider him good-looking. He had a small scar above his right cheek and straight white teeth. Ree couldn't quite pinpoint what it was about him—the air of a creep or criminal, or both— that made her want to be as far away as possible, but it was her job to find out.

"The people seem nice and the tips were better than I've ever made," she said.

Charley took a step back and smiled. "Good. See you in an hour for a double shift."

An hour? She couldn't imagine turning around and doing this again with a longer shift. Then again, it gave her an excuse to spend more time here.

"One of my waitresses called in sick," he explained. "Do you mind coming back?"

"Sure," she said before he walked back to the kitchen.

Ree topped off the last ketchup bottle and checked out. Sweat practically dripped off her as she made the walk next door, a wad of cash in her pocket. The money was good at Greenlight Bar and Restaurant. If she'd made this kind of cash in three hours at lunch, she could only imagine how much she could make at dinner. None of it was hers to keep, though.

As she approached the cabin, the door swung open. Her nerves tingled at seeing Quint again, but she told herself it was only because of the kiss earlier. And since she always faced her fears, she walked straight up to him before he could say a word and planted the steamiest kiss smack on the man's lips.

Her breath quickened, her heart raced and her body hummed with electricity. There was one question on her mind. Had she gone too far?

Chapter Three

The feel of Ree's lips pressed to Quint's reminded him of just how long it had been since he'd been with a woman. Not good. His last relationship hadn't ended well when he'd been accused of being in love with his former partner. Former dead partner now.

Ree brought her hands up to his shoulders as her tongue probed the inside of his mouth. Her touch was the equivalent of a bomb detonating inside his chest. Again, not good.

Quint let Ree have her moment. At least, that was the lie he told himself. Admitting she'd knocked him off balance meant he was so far off his game there was no coming back.

Pulling on all the willpower he had, Quint peeled her fingers off his shoulders and broke contact. They both heaved for air as though they'd just sprinted two blocks in the Texas heat.

Realizing the door was wide-open, he sidestepped Ree and closed it. And then the reason for the kiss dawned on him.

"You proved your point," he conceded.

She whirled around and poked her index finger in his chest. "Don't ever doubt whether or not I'm capable of doing my job again."

Her eyes were still glittery and he took some solace in the fact the kiss had shaken her as much as it had him, at least on the surface. He put his hands in the air in the surrender position, palms out. "I needed to know you were capable of going the distance if the case called for it."

"Yeah? How did I do?" she asked, issuing a challenge with those incredible green eyes of hers.

"I think we both know the answer to that question." He motioned toward one of the chairs at the two-top table in the kitchen area. "This might be a good time to get better acquainted."

"Sorry." She toed off a high heel, and then the second. A little mewl escaped when her feet were finally free. He'd heard the same sound when their lips had first touched. Twice kissed and they hadn't even gotten through their first day. It had to be a department record. "But I have to be back there in—" she checked her watch "—fifty-five minutes."

"What? Why?" He didn't bother to hide his shock.

"To work the dinner shift," she said, walking over to the couch instead of where he'd instructed.

"There has to be a law against overworking employees." He joined her in the living space, taking the chair across from her. The cabin's decor could best be described as simple. The sofa lined one wall and there were two chairs and a coffee table to create a sitting area. A rug defined the perimeter. Creaky, original wood flooring ran the entire open-concept room. A queen-size bed was tucked in another corner, affording very little privacy.

"Charley was already down one waitress and someone called in sick," she said.

"What was your impression of him?" Quint asked.

"He's a sexist jerk, for one." The fact she didn't hesitate meant there'd been some kind of run-in. Then again, he'd seen the tight-fitting uniforms. Quint fisted his hands thinking about a guy like Davies making a move on Ree. She seemed to realize how little clothing she had on at the mention of the guy, buttoning up her blouse and untying the bottom so she could wear it like a real shirt instead of a glorified swimsuit.

"Did he try anything with you?" Quint managed to ask through clenched teeth. The fact his protective instincts flared only served to remind him that he hadn't been able to distance himself from the memory of Tessa.

"Nothing like that," she said. "Just trying to get a feel for the guy."

"You must be tired after that shift. There's Coke in the fridge. Or I can put on a pot of coffee," he offered.

"Coke would be nice. Thanks." She started to get up, but he stopped her with a hand up, waving her off.

"This one's on me," he said as he stood. He retrieved two bottles, popped the caps and then set them down on the glass coffee table.

"Where'd you get these?" She picked hers up. Her forehead wrinkled with the question and it was about the sweetest thing he'd ever seen. It wouldn't be difficult to fake an attraction to someone like her: bold, intelligent and naturally beautiful.

"Corner store." This wasn't the time to get caught up in all things Ree Sheppard. Memorizing her quirks would help him down the line when he needed to know what she was thinking. Besides, those were the little things couples knew about each other. Those oddities that made up a person. Like the way she twisted a strand of hair in between her finger and thumb when she was thinking. Or the little concern line that scored her forehead when she was afraid she'd made a mistake.

Yes, he'd sat at the restaurant long enough to watch her when she was too busy to notice. And then, he'd exited before he could be identified. During the lunch rush, it had been easy to get in and out while staying under the radar. But Charley would have made note if Quint had stuck around. The bar owner might have already, which would say a whole lot about him and his character. Someone who constantly sized others up probably had something to hide. There was no doubt weapons were going through the back door at Greenlight. But who was involved?

"The other waitresses seem intimidated by him," Ree finally said after taking a few drinks from her Coke. She tucked a stray hair behind her ear, which he'd noticed meant it was time to get serious.

"It's possible he runs a tight ship. It's one way to keep his staff minding their own business," he said. Again, his hands fisted at the uncertainty of it all. They were going to have to work with another agency on this case most likely at some point. The realization brought all the flashbacks to mind. His blood boiled as he thought about the mistakes made on the night he'd lost his best friend, and remembered that she'd asked him to be the godfather of her kid. He still couldn't figure out how she'd talked him into holding off on telling their boss about the pregnancy. She'd asked for time to deliver the news on her own terms. And Quint would spend the rest of his life regretting giving in to her request. Because she and her baby would be alive right now if he'd stood his ground the first time. Tessa would have been assigned to desk duty and he would have gone into the bust alone.

"Everything okay?" Ree's voice broke through the memory.

"Yes. Fine. Never better." Quint shook it off. "What did you say before?"

She shot a look, and her forehead wrinkled.

"I stood up to him," she admitted. "I'm not sure he's used to getting that reaction from his waitresses."

"It could make him watch you closer." Quint didn't normally have an issue with keeping his temper under control. But right now, regrets about that other assignment sent his blood pressure soaring and gave him an intense need to put his fist through a wall. Better yet, find a boxing ring and go a couple of rounds with a willing participant.

Quint released a sharp sigh. Keeping his thoughts out of the past was proving more difficult than he'd imagined it would be.

He reminded himself this case was no different than the dozens of others he'd been on, and he could handle whatever came his way. Questioning himself on the fact would only lead to second-guessing himself in a critical moment. Ree deserved a partner with open eyes and a clear head.

"I SHOULD FEED you before you have to get back," Quint said and, for the first time, looked more concerned than angry at her.

"The food next door is amazing based on what I've seen and smelled. I get a dinner break, so I should be fine until then." Ree tucked her feet underneath her bottom as she finished the last of the Coke. It was exactly what she needed. That, and a few minutes to refresh her makeup before she headed back into the lion's den. The same nervous excitement struck every time she was about to go deep undercover.

"What have you done so far?" Quint reclaimed his seat.

"In terms of…?"

"Work assignments?" he asked.

"I'd rather talk about *this* one first, if you don't mind." Those last few words came out defensive, so she took in a slow breath to calm her nerves. Partnering with someone like Quint, with his formidable reputation, had a way of ramping up her nervous system. She had to remind herself she'd been assigned because she was ready for a case with the legend. She was going to make mistakes. Period. In life. In this job. Mistakes were inevitable. Granddad had once told her it wasn't the fact that she'd made a mistake that was important. It was the way she recovered that mattered.

Recovery was everything.

"That's fair," Quint said. "I was trying to get a gauge on whether or not you'd dealt with any weapons cases to see if we could find any links."

"None recently," she said.

"We both had access to the same file, so I know the basics about you," he continued.

Why did her stomach flip-flop at the thought Quinton Casey knew *anything* about her personal life? Or was it the lack of one that had her wishing she could sweep the whole topic under the rug?

"Ditto," she said.

"As far as this case goes, we know what we're looking for," he said.

"Any signs of weapons being run through the restaurant or via Charley, an employee or his suppliers," she said.

"The question isn't whether or not it's happening. We know that part is true after busting Lionel Turner," he continued after nodding his approval.

"Too bad he didn't give us names," she said.

"That would make this a little too simple for me," he countered.

She nodded. Right. The department wouldn't send someone like him for such easy pickings. Or her, for that matter.

He pulled a document up on his cell phone. "Greenlight has a total of five kitchen crew—a cook, two assistants, an expeditor and a dishwasher."

She nodded.

"Did you get any names?" he asked.

"One goes by Chef. The two assistants are Pele and Craig. The expeditor goes by Fender, and the dishwasher is Eddie."

He nodded as she rattled off names. "Chef must be Lorenzo Rocco, according to IRS payroll." He cocked an eyebrow. "Fender must be Alec Feeny."

"No idea what the real names are," she admitted.

"Waitresses are harder to identify since he only shows two on payroll," Quint stated.

A moment of silence passed. His forehead wrinkled.

"My favorite color is orange," he said, circling back to their earlier conversation. "Not like a pumpkin but like the burnt orange of a perfect sunset. When it feels like you're looking straight into a fire and are mesmerized by the orange glow."

"Burnt orange sunset. I got it." In fact, after the way he described it, she didn't think she'd ever forget it. She also liked that he was telling her something about himself that most people wouldn't know or be able to guess. Her heart gave a little squeeze in what felt like a strangely intimate moment happening between them.

"Pizza any day over a burger and my favorite beer is whatever is on tap," he continued. "I like those pizzas where the chef throws together ingredients that maybe shouldn't work together but somehow do."

"There's a place on Third Street in Austin that has the best craft pizza. Ronnie always comes out to the table when the special is ordered," she said.

"I know Ronnie." He quirked a brow. "You know Ronnie?"

"Not exactly *know* him. But I do know his pizzas and they are hands down the best in the state," she said, unable to contain the excitement in her voice.

"That's where I took you on our first date, then," he said with a glimmer in his eyes that caused her stomach to free-fall.

"It was a perfect night," she said, continuing on with the cover.

"I knew the minute you ordered the special you were different," he said. His eyes lit up. His expression softened. The way he spoke about their fake date almost like it was real was incredibly sexy. "I never believed in love at first sight but I sensed you were going to be important in my life."

Well, now she really was transfixed.

"The same was true for me," she said. "There was something about sharing that first slice that made my whole future flash before my eyes. Us. Kids. A house."

Quint cleared his throat, as if it had suddenly

dried up. He took a swig of his Coke before setting the bottle down on the coffee table and glancing at the clock on the wall. "You have to head out in ten minutes. I think we've got enough for now."

"Yeah. Right." Ree forced her gaze away from him. She pushed up to standing and oriented herself toward the bathroom. Something was missing. It didn't take long to figure out what it was. "Right. What was I thinking? My suitcase is in the trunk. I'll just go—"

"I got it." He waved her off.

"Not so fast." She rounded the coffee table in time to grab him by the arm. He whirled around a little too fast and the heat of his stare caused her breath to catch. She swallowed to ease some of the dryness in her throat.

The look he gave her could have melted an iceberg.

"Your ankle," she managed to get out. "How will it look if you bring in my suitcases when you're supposed to be hurt."

He stared at her, boldly, unapologetically. He had to know she was right and yet he didn't seem ready to accept it. Someone like him, young and strong, would have a hard time leaving her to her own devices. Turned out chivalry wasn't dead. She'd witnessed it too many times in her home state where men opened doors for women. Not because a woman couldn't do it for herself, but because he followed a code that said, ladies first.

"All right," he finally grunted out. "But I'm helping because if I don't and Charley's watching he won't buy into the newlywed angle."

"Sounds good," she said. "I'll make a show of forcing you to let me take my own suitcase."

"That'll help." His face still looked pinched at the prospect of leaving her to it.

"And the story is still that you are studying to get certification in the computer field after being hurt on a job with your moving company, right?" she asked.

"The injury is the last straw since I'm not twenty anymore," he said with a nod. "At forty-two, I realized that I needed a desk job."

"And I'm going to be the one working and supporting you while you finish your studies," she confirmed.

"That's right. We're also looking to pare down expenses now and are ready for a change from big-city life," he said with an approving smile. One that shouldn't send her heart fluttering.

It dawned on Ree that she could use her body's reaction to sell the newlywed bit. Her cheeks flushed unintentionally when Quint put his full attention on her. She could use it to her benefit rather than constantly fight against her biology.

There was no use belaboring the point about who carried the bag inside. They were making progress on the rules-of-engagement front, on the getting-to-know-the-little-things front and on the working-together front. She would take the progress as she excused herself. She walked out to her car, if it could be called that considering how bad a shape it was in, and popped open the trunk.

Quint lifted the suitcase out as she insisted on helping. Thankfully, it was on rollers despite the gravel parking lot. She threw her arms around his neck, and quickly realized how much the move caused her breasts to press against the wall of his muscled chest.

For the second time her breath caught, her heart hammered her ribs, and an urge to kiss him overwhelmed her senses. She could do this assignment without getting personally attached…right?

Chapter Four

"Why did you show up at work, by the way?" Ree asked, following Quint inside.

Honesty was probably the best policy, so he didn't hide the truth. "I was concerned about you when you didn't return."

Her eyebrow shot up as she kneeled and then opened her suitcase. She located a small floral bag with a zipper, and then walked to the bathroom. "You didn't trust me?"

"I didn't trust him." He nodded toward the restaurant as he followed. "I didn't know you."

Both statements were true. Neither covered his real motivation. Guilt stabbed him for the way he'd treated her and he was doing his level best to shake off his mistakes with the Tessa case.

"Fair enough," she finally said.

"I owe you an apology," he continued. "You can write me up for the kiss if you'd like. I promise that I do know how to respect boundaries even if it means—"

"We're newlyweds," she said, putting a hand up to stop him. "And they kiss all the time. Believe me,

I've seen it with my brother. You were right to remind me of the fact. Besides, I could have walked away at any time. You need to know that you can trust me to do what is necessary and I didn't back away in order to prove to you that I can. You weren't wrong. I was."

"I'll do my best to minimize physical contact," he offered.

"You better not. Go watch any newly married couple. We might blow our cover," she said, fixing her gaze on the mirror as she freshened up her makeup. As far as he was concerned, she looked perfect.

He couldn't tear his gaze away as she pulled out a small round metal tin. After unscrewing the top, she dabbed her pinkie finger into the container and then dotted her lips with a light pink gloss.

Quint swallowed to ease the sudden dryness in his throat. The surge of attraction was a normal reaction to being in close proximity to an intelligent, beautiful woman. Nothing more. This was proof Quint wasn't off his game even if it was misguided. Where was a reset button when he needed one?

Ree squirted her hair with something that made it look even more silky, and a stab of jealousy knifed him in the chest that she was making herself more beautiful to walk next door. How was that for keeping his cool?

"Do you have any brothers or sisters?" she asked out of the blue.

"None that I know of," he said. "My dad didn't exactly keep in touch when he left me and my mom to our own devices."

"Oh." She immediately reached over and touched his hand, a simple gesture that meant a lot to him. "I'm really sorry."

"We survived all right without him." He heard the defensiveness in his own voice. "Which is to say she worked two jobs to support us and I was a total jerk until I found my way."

"That must have been hard on you," she said. The compassion in her voice touched him in a place long forgotten.

Ree checked the time and gasped.

"I'm sorry. I have to go." Her eyes pleaded forgiveness.

"I'll walk you over," he said, shaking off the moment happening between them. "It'll give me a chance to check out the vehicles in the parking lot again. Plus, it won't hurt if Charley sees you with your husband. We need to find a way to work me into the conversation and possibly figure out how to get me on his computer."

In part, Quint wanted to make a statement to the man that she was off-limits, and he also needed to make himself known to her boss. Charley would be seeing Quint around, and it was time to lay the groundwork.

"Okay," she said before turning and wrapping her arms around his neck. When her green eyes met his, he took another hit square in the chest.

He peeled her arms off him.

"What was that for?" he asked, hearing the huskiness in his own voice.

"Practice," she said, almost beaming.

"Right." He coughed, thinking there were a few other marital things he'd like to be doing right now with Ree. Since those thoughts were as productive as digging in dry Texas dirt with a hand trowel, he shelved them.

Quint gave himself a mental slap and forced a smile. "Ready?"

"As much as I'll ever be," she admitted with wide, beautiful eyes. He could see the same mix of excitement and fear he experienced on a new case. Now he got more of the adrenaline rush—some might even call him an adrenaline junkie—but not so much of the excitement, since Tessa. This career was it for him, though. It was the job he'd trained for. The job he'd expected to still be doing and loving for years down the line. And the one he planned to get a pension from.

In short, it was all he knew how to do.

The pair walked across the parking lot, hand in hand. He discreetly checked license plates. Quint stopped at the glass doors where it would be easy for anyone to see him from inside the place. "This is where I make my exit."

There weren't a whole lot of cars yet. It was probably too early for the dinner crowd. A truck pulled up as Ree repeated the same move from the bathroom earlier, throwing her arms around his neck. He didn't want to notice how right she felt pressed against his body or how firm her breasts were when they were flush against him.

Instead of overthinking his physical reaction, he looped his arms around her waist, dipped his head and kissed her.

"See you at home tonight," she said, slowly opening eyes that glittered with something that looked a lot like need.

If she was acting, she deserved an award.

"I might be by for a late dinner," he said as a couple walked behind them. Since small towns usually spread word around and he didn't know the players yet, he added, "Once I get my homework finished."

"Then, I'll see you before my shift is over," she said, throwing him a smile that radiated.

What was he supposed to do with that? There was an innocence and determination in her eyes that he hadn't seen in a long time, not in others and not in himself.

"Bye." He feathered a kiss on her lips before she took off without looking back.

He just stood there for a long moment wondering what in the heck had just happened to him.

Shaking it off, he turned and made his way back to the cabin. Once there, he opened the blinds. There was enough sun outside to light the cabin. Plus, he wanted to snap a couple of pictures as vehicles showed up, start the process of figuring out who the regulars were versus those just driving through town or stopping off specifically to eat there.

Within the hour, the lot was full. Quint snapped a pic of the activity, zeroing in on faces when possible. He needed to get to know the locals and this was the best way. Plus, he could have home base run facial recognition software if he could get a good shot on a suspect.

Curiosity had him pulling Ree's file out of his backpack. He skimmed the contents, noting her marital status as single. He should have asked earlier, telling himself he needed to know for the assignment rather than for personal knowledge. He couldn't deny the relief that washed over him at the realization she wasn't married. Then again, she might have a boyfriend or a significant other. People didn't have to be married to be in a committed relationship. Although, he wouldn't know. After a bad breakup in his early twenties he'd decided not to touch that stove again.

Besides, he'd had all the company and friendship he could want from work, with Tessa as a partner. The two of them had done everything together when she was alive. Dinners? Check. Beer and sports nights? Check. Paintball wars on days off? Check.

They would spark romance rumors from time to time, but anyone who really knew them realized they were best friends and nothing more. Not the kind of romantic best friends that made for a good marriage, either. Just two buddies who got each other and enjoyed hanging out. There were discussions about the need to back off the friendship when one or both of them got involved in a relationship, and they did. Their baseline had always been mutual respect and giving space when needed.

The formula worked and eased the pinch when

either one ended a fling. It could be a relief in many cases when a date went south because Quint always knew he could call Tessa and grab a beer. Until Tessa started drinking water out of nowhere, like he wouldn't notice. She covered by complaining about an ulcer. The excuse had bought her a little more time.

Quint stayed lost in thought longer than he'd intended. By the time he shook out of the haze of memories it was time to head next door. Before leaving, he closed the mini blinds and sneaked in a few more shots of the parking lot. He sent those to headquarters, so Agent Grappell could run the plates.

Taking and sending pictures every night would give him a sense of who the regulars were. Now it was time to pack up, hide the files and see what this Charley person looked like in the flesh.

REE HAD KEPT one eye on the door all evening before she caught herself doing it. The night so far had been one big dinner rush. But it was dark outside now and the tables were thinning, while the bar area was starting to hop instead.

Live-music Thursdays would bring a band tomorrow night. She could only imagine what that might do for business considering how lively it had been tonight. And it was only a Wednesday. The specials had looked and smelled amazing all evening. Of course, after working here for a while she would probably get sick of it all.

"Hey, table five is looking ready for their check," Adrian said as she buzzed past.

"Thank you," Ree said to the veteran waitress. Ree had literally gone to the bathroom for five seconds.

She dropped off a check as she heard the door open behind her and a familiar voice call her name.

"Ree Sheppard?" Sarah Combs's voice sent a shock wave down Ree's back.

Ree spun around to face Sarah and Marcus Brown.

"What are you doing here?" Ree stared into the very brown eyes of someone she'd gone to high school with in the small town where she grew up outside of Houston, and her youngest brother's best friend. "And when did you two start going out?"

"Heard the food is top shelf here," Sarah said, then held up her wedding finger. "We've been married five years now. We have two kids who are with my parents this weekend. We're on a road trip and heard about the food here. This is so crazy. What are the odds? We just went out with your brother last weekend. Didn't we, Marcus?"

Marcus nodded.

"I'm Matthews now." Ree could feel the blood rush to her cheeks as she displayed her wedding band. She heard a whoosh sound in her ears. She had to finagle a way out of this before Adrian or Zoey caught on.

"Are you okay?" Sarah asked, twisting her face up.

"Yes. Of course. Just surprised to see y'all. Why don't you guys sit over here in my station where we can catch up in between customers," Ree said, motioning toward a booth along the opposite wall from the bar. "The crowd is slowing down and I want to hear about the kids."

"Okay, but I'm so confused. How are you a waitress? Your brother just said you worked in—"

Ree shot Sarah a look that could cut through steel. Marcus wrapped his arm around his wife's shoulder and mouthed an apology. He led Sarah to the booth Ree had indicated a few seconds ago.

The hairs on Ree's neck pricked as fear washed over her. She cleared her throat and turned around in time to see Zoey staring. Did she suspect something?

Was Ree's cover blown?

A pair of guys walked in the door. One was tall, bald, and wore a leather biker jacket. The other was short and round-bellied, with a full head of hair and ruddy cheeks. They were an odd pairing and the kind of people trouble usually followed.

"Table for two?" she asked as Zoey lingered at a nearby table.

Ruddy motioned toward the bar.

"Live music is tomorrow. Thursday. Bar closes early on Wednesdays," she informed him. The look she received in return could freeze alcohol.

"Go ahead and take a seat," she urged, motioning toward the bar. "I'll grab Charley."

Ruddy nodded.

Rather than give in to full-scale panic, she grabbed two waters from the back and brought them out to her new table. "Menus are right here." She pointed. "I'll be right back."

Ree needed to find Charley and let him know

his "friends" were in the house. She darted to the kitchen. "Has anyone seen Charley?"

Chef was retying his apron. He glanced up. "Cold storage, maybe?"

Ree crossed the room to cold storage and located Charley sitting on a stack of boxes, staring at a tablet. He was most likely doing inventory.

"Hey, Charley. A couple of guys are here. I think they're friends of yours. They're insisting on sitting in the bar area even though I told them it was closed," she said.

A momentary look of fear flashed across Charley's face. His muscles tensed before he took in a breath and looked up from his tablet.

"Should I serve the table?" she asked, noting his reaction.

"I'll handle it," he said in a world-weary voice. "Just see if you can get them anything to drink and tell them I'll be right there."

"Will do," she said before making a hasty exit. Could she still save the situation with Sarah?

As she crossed the kitchen, she saw Adrian whispering to Zoey. What was that all about? This investigation was crumbling right before her eyes. Sarah and Marcus's timing couldn't be worse, and the pair of men in the bar needed watching.

She hurried to Marcus and Sarah's table. He was on the phone in an animated conversation.

"We'll be home shortly, Mom," he said. "Tell the kids to stop crying. We'll be there to tuck them in."

Sarah's face was pinched. She whispered, "We have to go. Sorry."

"Are you sure?" Ree asked, trying to sell the lie they'd just met in case someone was listening. "The food here is top-notch."

"Yeah, no, sorry," Sarah said a little loudly. "It's the kids."

Marcus ended the call as they left the booth. "We'll come back another time."

"Okay," Ree said, her heart racing. "Suit your self."

As the two left, she glanced toward the bar and saw him. Quint. He sat across the bar from Ruddy and Bald. Her stomach flip-flopped and her breath caught at the sight of her partner. He had the kind of rugged good looks that said he could handle him-self in just about any situation, which only added to his sex appeal.

He sat on a barstool, finishing a beer, looking a little too good in his jeans and button-down. Be still, her heart.

It was probably naive to think she could surprise him, considering not much seemed to get past the man. This time seemed no exception as she walked up behind him. He reached back, grabbed her hand and squeezed before letting it go without missing a beat.

Someone would have to be watching to catch what had happened and when she glanced around, she saw Charley staring at them from the mouth of the hallway that led to the restroom, his gaze bouncing from her and Quint to his visitors. His expression could best be described as interested as he seemed to study them. Even from this distance, she could see his frown. Had they crossed a line?

Chapter Five

Rather than guess, she walked right over to Charley with a wide smile. "That's the husband I was telling you about on break earlier."

"Oh, really?" Charley's eyebrows knitted together.

"It's okay if he comes here to eat, right? We can pay for his dinner if that's a—"

Charley shook his head.

"No problem. Family gets the employee discount. Make sure Stevie knows." Charley nodded toward Quint. "I'd keep an eye on your man around here if I were you."

Ree turned around in time to see the female bartender throwing her hair back, laughing, and making conversation with Quint as she closed down the bar. A twinge of jealousy formed a knot in her stomach.

"Didn't realize I would have to," she said, trying to joke. It fell flat.

"No physical contact while you're working. It's bad for business," Charley said before walking away and heading into the kitchen.

Ree stood there for a long moment.

"Don't worry," Adrian said as she walked over. "Charley is all bark and no bite."

"He's serious about the no-touching policy, though. Isn't he?" she asked, not needing to fake disappointment.

"At first, I'd toe the line if I were you. Give it a few weeks and he'll lighten up," Adrian said. "Charley usually takes a shine to the new girls, so he probably doesn't love the fact you're married."

Ree decided this wasn't the time to mention that she wasn't a "girl." Adrian probably hadn't intentionally been offensive. "Are you saying he has a crush on me?"

"You wouldn't be the first," Adrian said. "He's gone out with several of us."

Ree picked up on the *us* immediately. She didn't need to be a good investigator to realize Adrian had dated Charley. Had Zoey done the same?

"It's all fun and games in the beginning," the other waitress continued wistfully. "He can be quite a charmer when he puts his mind to it."

"And when he doesn't?" Ree asked more out of curiosity than anything else. This information was painting a picture of the man who ran Greenlight, and Ree needed all the information she could get.

"Let's just say it gets real cold in the shadows," Adrian said.

Ree nodded toward Zoey. "What about her? Did they date?"

"I'm not sure what to think about poor Zoey," Adrian said, moving closer and whispering.

"Not cool." Ree figured Charley could go down on at least one charge even if he wasn't responsible for the guns running out of the back of his establishment. At the very least, he needed to learn how to respect women.

Adrian shrugged. "She's young and doesn't talk much. I know she's staying at the motel a couple of blocks from here. It's one of those pay-by-the-week places."

"Any family around?" Ree figured she needed to let it go, so this would be the last question. She didn't need to snap into investigator mode.

"Just the jerk over there at the bar. He used to show up more, yelling at her in the parking lot," Adrian said, making a face.

"Poor kid." Ree shook her head. "She can't be more than twenty."

"Yeah," Adrian agreed. "What's your story?"

Ree gave her the two-minute version before excusing herself to check on an order from the kitchen. Adrian had handed over interesting information about Zoey. When Ree really looked at the other waitress, she thought Adrian might have a point about age. Zoey could pass for twenty but she might barely be eighteen. There were some very physically mature teenagers who looked much older than they were. Puberty could be an interesting mixer. Ree fell into the late bloomer camp and she'd always been told she looked younger than she really was. She figured she'd appreciate it later in life. Not so much after she'd turned twenty-one and was constantly carded while ordering a beer after work or trying to buy a bottle of wine on her way home.

After setting down plates, she made rounds. Table three needed their check, so she handled that. More water for table two, so she fixed that easily enough.

At least they'd made it through a night. Everything hurt after being on her feet all day. Time to close up the restaurant side couldn't come fast enough. The scare with Sarah and Marcus had her nerves on edge.

After filling her last ketchup bottle, she got her handbag out of the locker she'd been assigned in back. The room wasn't much larger than a walk-in pantry with space for no more than three people at one time. The back door was beside it and a small employee bathroom sat directly across. Ree took special note of the layout, and the camera positioned above the back door.

Quint was no longer sitting at the bar by the time she reentered the dining room, but Charley was in deep conversation with Ruddy and Bald. A moment of panic struck as she scanned the room. He probably headed back to the cabin without her. They hadn't exactly come up with a plan for how to handle nights. Still, for reasons she didn't want to examine, it bothered her that he hadn't stayed to walk her home.

Mentally shaking it off, she said good-night to the others and headed out the front door.

Quint was there, sitting, and her heart gave a little flip. He stood up the minute she walked outside.

"Hey," he said, dipping his head down and kissing her before linking their fingers. Heat swirled through her body. Instead of fighting the feeling, she leaned into it.

"How was work?" he asked, giving her hand a little squeeze.

This might just be for show but there was something nice about him being there.

"Good tips tonight but my feet are ready to fall off," she admitted.

"Too bad I have this injury or I'd carry you over the threshold," he said and she couldn't tell if he was serious or joking as they headed home to the cabin. He lowered his voice when he said, "I have information."

Ree's mind immediately snapped to Ruddy and Bald. Then there was Zoey. The young woman was on her mind now and she couldn't shake the feeling of wanting to help.

QUINT LET GO of Ree's hand the minute they were safely inside the cabin. He instantly felt cold where warmth used to be. "Charley's cousin is the sheriff."

"Interesting. I don't remember seeing that intel in the brief." Ree kicked off her boots at the door and walked over to the sofa before plopping down. She started rubbing her feet almost immediately.

"They had different last names and there's a step-family situation, which took the agency a minute to figure out," he stated, walking over to the fridge. "Do you want anything to drink?"

"Water would be nice. I had fifteen minutes to

gobble down my dinner, which was the most amazing chicken-fried steak I've ever eaten, and almost no time to stay hydrated." She groaned her pleasure at the mention of the food and it wasn't a sound he needed to have associated with her.

He might have had doubts about being able to work with Ree but he was coming around. She'd held her own on a long shift and, in his estimation, had to do the heavy lifting in the case by working at Greenlight.

Quint poured two glasses of water and brought hers over to the coffee table, setting it down within arm's reach.

"Thank you," she said. "Interesting about the sheriff. Did you get his or her name?"

"Sheriff Welton Rice," Quint supplied.

"I'm sure the agency is doing a deep dive into his background," she said. "Seeing if he has any blemishes on his record."

He nodded. She was on the right track. He dimmed the lights before taking a seat across from her.

"I'm sure you took note of the two men who came in at closing time," she stated.

"The bald guy and the one with the ruddy complexion," he said. "Hard to miss those two."

"And the fact my cover was almost blown by my brother's friends." She gave him a quick rundown. "I don't think anyone caught on but I did see Adrian and Zoey whispering."

"Could have been about anything," he said.

"I know. The timing is terrible, though," she said.

"It's never a good time to run into people from your real world," he stated. "I can feel Stevie out to see if you hit her radar. She keeps tabs on what goes on at the place."

"You definitely hit Charley's radar," she said as a look flashed behind her eyes. If they were a real couple, he'd say it was jealousy. Under the circumstances, it couldn't be.

"What did he say?" he asked.

"No touching. Said it's bad for business," she stated. "You can swing by for dinner. I get the impression he doesn't mind as long as we steer clear of each other inside those glass doors."

"Got it," he said. "The man keeps a close eye."

"He's either very involved at running his business or has something to hide," she said.

He nodded. The two of them were hitting a stride with each other.

"Mind if I ask a personal question?" he asked, trying to capitalize on the comfort they were developing with their partnership.

"Go ahead." She picked up the water and took a sip.

"Why did you get into law enforcement?" he asked. Everyone he'd come across, be it cop, agent or investigator, had a story.

"Um, well…" She seemed a little surprised by the change in direction. "Let's see, I grew up with four brothers thinking I was one of them, so I was never going to be a prima ballerina, much to my mother's great shock and disappointment."

"Expectations are hard to live up to. I can't imagine what it must have been like to come from such a big family, though," he said. "To be honest, I always wished for siblings."

"Mine are all great in their own ways and they never treated me like I was anything less than an equal," she admitted with a smile. "But I followed in my dad's footsteps going into law enforcement. He was killed in a high-speed chase when I was little, so my grandfather stepped in. He was always my role model and hero." The note of melancholy in her voice said she missed her father very much.

"What made you decide law enforcement was the right career?" he asked.

"Why does anyone follow in anyone else's footsteps. To make them proud, I guess. It's in the blood for me," she admitted. "What about you?"

"Okay," he started. She'd been honest with him, so reciprocating was the least he could do. "You already know that I grew up with a single mother who worked two jobs. We lived in a trailer park on the outskirts of Houston and she was gone most of the time. I got bored. Lonely. So I got into trouble."

She winced before taking another sip. "Must have turned out okay since you're here. What happened?"

"There was a liaison officer at my school who realized I needed a male role model in my life," he said, thinking that he never told this story. "His name was Officer Jazz, so, clearly, we used fake dance behind his back. Jazz hands and all."

She laughed and it was the most musical sound.

"One of the times I got into trouble, he took it

upon himself to speak to the office about me. My teachers came forward saying I used to be a good student and they weren't sure what happened. Jazzy, as I used to call him, didn't leave it there. He kept digging and then eventually asked if he could sit with me at lunch one day. Said there was a program and wanted to know if I'd be his little brother," he said. "I balked at first but then I got into really bad trouble. I remember distinctly sitting across the dining room table from my mom and seeing the exhaustion and hurt in her eyes. She could barely stay awake because she'd worked all night at the hospital changing bedpans. It just clicked for me in that moment she deserved better from me."

"Your mom sounds like an amazing person," she said with so much admiration in her voice a place deep down inside him awakened, bringing a peek of light.

"She was," he said, covering the emotion building with the realization he never spoke about his mom to anyone. Not even Tessa.

"I'm so sorry." Ree's expression changed from admiration to sorrow.

"She got sick. It was a long time ago." Those were the mantras he repeated in order to shove his feelings aside.

"It sounds like you two were very close," she observed.

"Yes, and the point of the story is that having someone other than my mother believe in me, having Jazzy, made all the difference in the world. It saved my life," he said in a tone that revealed this conversation was changing directions.

Ree sat there for a long moment, looking lost in thought. "I wonder who Zoey has had in her life."

"The young waitress?" he asked.

"Yes. Adrian mentioned Zoey might be in a bad relationship and living with the guy in a motel down the street," she said.

"Think you can get close to her? Find out her story?" Quint asked, his own anger rising at the thought of a lost young person.

Ree nodded.

"It's just sad. You know?" She lifted those incredible green eyes to meet his. "She is still so young and it doesn't seem like she has anyone to look out for her."

He did know to a point. He'd never doubted his mom's love and it was the other reason he'd wanted to shift gears and be a better person all those years ago. Desire was one thing and a good place to start. Having support taught him how to cross the finish line.

"The boyfriend might be an abusive boyfriend," Ree said.

"We'll do what we can to help her no matter what else happens on this case," he promised, and he had every intention of following through. No young person should be left to their own devices when others could step in and offer a hand up. "Which doesn't mean she'll take it. We can't do anything for her. She has to be ready to leave him if that's the situation."

"We can try. This is good," Ree said, her eyes

lighting up. "What's the point of doing this job if we can't make a difference, right?"

Quint couldn't have said it better himself. Up until now, he'd viewed his job as taking bad guys off the streets. He realized how cliché it sounded early on in his career, so he didn't bring it up with other officers, or civilians for that matter. There'd been a few cases involving misguided young folks that had stuck with him. Maybe he and Ree could make a difference in this case.

He glanced at the clock. They'd been talking way too long and Ree needed to get some rest if she was going to do this all again tomorrow. They'd made good progress tonight toward getting to know each other and working together.

"What do you think about turning in for the night?" he asked.

Ree checked the time. "Oh, wow. I really lost track of time here."

She stood.

"I'm a night shower person, so I'll just grab my clothes. This sofa is fine with me for sleeping if you want to throw a blanket and pillow over here," she stated, biting back a yawn as though being reminded of her exhaustion suddenly kicked her body into sleep mode.

"I'll have everything ready for when you're done," he confirmed. There was no way he was letting her take the sofa when he could easily grab a nap during the day if needed.

Ree left the room as he thought about how little

he ever spoke about his mom. Tessa had stepped into the role of his only living family and he'd buried childhood memories down deep. Memories of how he and his mother used to have one meal a day together, his breakfast and her dinner. It was the half hour their lives crossed and they spent time talking, checking in with each other. Looking back, he could see those meals started happening after Jazzy came into their lives. Quint's mother had been seventeen when she'd given birth to him and, although he never doubted her love for him, she probably didn't have the necessary parenting skills.

This whole conversation with Ree reminded Quint to catch up with Jazzy, maybe take him out for a beer.

He shifted his thoughts back to the case. He needed to review the video footage from the pencil-sized cameras he'd placed in the windows. The recordings were feeding to his laptop and he needed to watch the footage so he could start getting a sense of routines and behaviors. Since he didn't have unlimited data storage and the Wi-Fi was sketchy out here, he would have to take notes and then erase the recordings on a regular basis. He opened his laptop and fired off an email to Agent Grappell about the sheriff's connection.

For the time being, he would have to mostly rely on intel Ree provided, since he hadn't gotten a toe in the door yet. It was early and these investigations could take weeks, even months when going deep undercover. Considering they already knew weapons were being run out the back, this one should be on the shorter side. Why did the thought hold less appeal now that he was getting to know Ree?

For the first time since this whole case began, he didn't balk at the idea of being with another female partner. Ree had proved she could stand up to him, which was important. She'd more than proved she could handle the job next door. Her waitressing skills looked on point when he was in the room and she'd already scored critical pieces of information and that was just on day one. Charley seemed to have taken a shine to her. As much as Quint didn't like that part, she'd played her hand perfectly with the restaurant owner, proving to be a valuable asset while under pressure.

For the first time since losing Tessa, Quint was warming up to working with a new partner. Now it was time to check out the camera footage and see what else he could find.

REE FINISHED HER shower in record time, exhaustion having settled in the minute she peeled off her work clothes. She would get two uniforms so she could wear one and wash the other. Thankfully, she'd seen a washer/dryer combo in the hall closet. The embarrassment of her undergarments being hung outside for the world to see wasn't exactly something she could digest at the moment. She didn't exactly want Quint handling her bra and panties, either.

The day had been productive for a first day. Groundwork was being laid. She'd established a few boundaries and Quint had been introduced to the picture. This was all good progress.

Ree toweled off, and dressed in the most innocuous pair of pajamas known to man: lounge pants and an oversize T-shirt. She secured a light robe on top as if the other pieces weren't figure-hiding enough. Besides, she was a tornado when she slept, so she needed coverage. She threw her uniform and day's undergarments into the washer and turned it on.

Walking into the living room, she noticed the sofa bed had been pulled out. She started toward it when Quint practically growled at her to take the bed.

"Why? What changed in the last fifteen minutes since I was in the shower?" she asked.

"You need a good night's sleep." He pointed to the sofa bed. "That thing isn't going to give it to you."

"With all due respect, the same is true for you," she said, standing her ground.

"I can sleep sitting up if needed, and take a nap if I crash in the daytime. You, on the other hand, have to be on your feet all day again tomorrow. Do you want to do that after sleeping with a rod up your back?" he asked, not looking up from his laptop.

"When you put it that way, no," she admitted. "But I don't need you to make concessions for me because I'm fem—"

"I wasn't," came the growl that practically shook the walls.

"Good," she shot back, forcing herself to be unafraid. She'd seen his gentle side when he spoke about his mom. A good person was behind those steel walls he'd erected. After learning about his background, she understood him better. She also realized her brother Shane was right. She had to be brave if she was ever going to have a chance to break down Quint's barriers. A voice in the back of her head told her that he wasn't the type to share his past easily or with many. The moment that had happened between them was special, and despite initial evidence to the contrary, the two of them might just end up friends.

The same voice picked that moment to remind her that friends didn't cause electricity to pulse through her at the lightest contact or her stomach to free-fall with a glance in her direction.

She shelved those thoughts under the category of *unproductive.*

Quint's reputation said he was one of the best at his job. She intended to use this time to learn from a master because who knew when an opportunity like this would ever come along again? Being paired with an agent like Quint was a dream come true.

"You want me to sleep on the bed? I'll take the bed," she said, throwing her arms up like it didn't matter one way or the other to her. "I don't mind being comfortable and this mattress looks like a dream."

It didn't. But she didn't let that stop her from singing its praises.

Quint didn't respond. After growing up with four brothers, she realized she'd scored a direct hit.

"Bathroom is yours," she said, climbing under

the sheets. She checked her cell before going to bed and saw there was a text from Preston. Hey, was all it said. She wasn't touching that one with a ten-foot pole. The last time she responded to one of her ex's texts a six-week fling had kicked off. Granted, the sex had been worth it, but walking away from him a second time had practically gutted her. Plus, she was on an assignment. The rest of the world had to wait. She didn't even contact her brothers when she was undercover.

The lights were dim enough for her to sleep. She'd never been especially picky in that department. All she needed was a bed, covers and AC in order to be good to go for a night's rest. And not even a good bed, which was the reason she'd volunteered to take the couch in the first place. It really didn't matter much to her and his sheer size should dictate he take the larger mattress. But hey, whatever he wanted was fine with her.

"Is Charley still hiring waitresses?" Quint asked.

"Not that I know of," she said. "Why?"

"I was trying to figure out the reason for the double shift and if this was going to be the norm," he said.

"A waitress called in sick. Normally, I'll be working the lunch shift but he needs me for both while she's out," she said.

"At least you'll get to know the players faster that way," he said.

Tomorrow, on her shift, she planned to keep a closer eye on Zoey as long as she could do it without getting caught. No matter how much her heart went out to Zoey, she couldn't become a distraction to the real assignment. Could she get the young woman to talk? Share her story?

Ree glanced at the clock. She would know in less than twelve hours.

Chapter Six

Sunshine was already peeking through the slats of the mini blinds when Ree's smartwatch buzzed. She sat bolt upright, trying to get her bearings.

"Morning." Quint's whiskey-on-ice voice poured over her and through her.

"Don't you ever sleep?" She squinted through blurry eyes as she yawned.

His chuckle was a low rumble in his chest. He pushed to standing from the chair and headed into the kitchen. A few seconds later, he returned with a coffee mug in hand.

"Thank you," she said, taking the offering and inhaling the smell of fresh brew.

"You're welcome." He reclaimed his seat and stared at his laptop. "I do sleep, by the way."

"Really?" She took a sip, welcoming the burn on her throat. "And this is amazing."

"Yes. Everyone does. Don't believe anyone who tries to convince you otherwise. I just came into this assignment well rested. I'm good for a few nights sleeping in short bursts."

"Gotcha. I'm more of a 'straight eight' type but can get by on six and a half when absolutely necessary. It gets ugly after that," she said with a smile. "Are you a robot?"

"Yes," he said, as serious as a pastor during Sunday morning church service. Then he picked up his own coffee mug and rewarded her with a smile in a show of perfectly straight, perfectly white teeth. Teeth were just the beginning of perfection on this man. Some might have considered the half-inch scar above his right eyebrow and other physical traits as flaws. Ree didn't fall into that camp. Those little things were precisely what set someone apart and made them even more attractive, gave them sex appeal as opposed to just being a beautiful shell. Personality influenced looks. She'd met plenty of beautiful-on-the-outside people whose looks deteriorated in her eyes once they opened their mouths to speak. Intelligence was sexy. A sense of humor... sexy.

"Oh, you actually have a sense of humor," she teased, thinking how nice it was to break some of the tension by joking around. Last night had thrown a lot at her at Greenlight. Based on the stress lines etched into his forehead, he didn't laugh nearly often enough and was as concerned about her going back today as she was. She knew his mother was gone and wondered if there'd been someone else special in his life that he'd lost.

Hold on a minute. It was coming back to her now. Didn't he use to work with someone who'd been killed on the job? Ree made a mental note to research that later. There would be news articles if an agent had been killed on duty. It was a big department but she'd heard about a female agent being killed in a bust after the New Year.

Setting the thought aside, she took another sip of coffee, figuring she needed to milk this morning before her day shifted into high gear.

"What are you studying on that thing?" she asked, hugging her knees into her chest.

"Video footage from the past—" he checked the time "—ten hours or so."

"Are you seeing anything worth talking about?" she asked.

"Not yet. I'm still getting the lay of the land so I can start memorizing routines, regular customers, delivery flow," he admitted. "I snapped a couple of faces to send to Grappell so he can run them through facial recognition software. See if we can get any hits there."

"Looking for patterns," she said. "How much data can that thing store?"

"Yes. And not enough to keep more than twenty-four hours of video on hand," he said.

"Of course, we don't need that much," she surmised.

"Nope. So I'm capturing screenshots of vehicles with their license plates, too. Sending everything to headquarters. There was a liquor delivery at ten o'clock last night that I recorded," he said. "I grabbed pictures of faces in the truck but I got side views and the pictures are grainy when I blow them up. There's enough there to see if the same delivery drivers worked the route but not to ID anyone."

"I'll try to work the back of the house a little more today. A camera is pointed directly at the back door." She grabbed a pen and notepad before drawing out the layout of Greenlight. "To be honest, yesterday was such a whirlwind that I didn't do a great job of getting to know the players in the kitchen," she admitted. "It's been a really long time since I was a waitress and I spent most of the time praying I wouldn't drop a tray while serving customers, and getting introduced to the other waitresses. I put most of my energy toward trying not to get fired my first day on the job. Then, we already know about Sarah and Marcus's visit."

She rolled the coffee mug around in her palms, appreciating the warmth after pushing the notepad toward Quint.

"It's too soon for me to approach Charley about helping out with his computer system," Quint said and she agreed. "This layout is helpful."

"I caught him staring at you from across the room last night," she said. "I meant to mention that before."

"Then I better back off today. Think you'll be okay?" he asked before seeming to catch himself.

"Yes," she said a little too defensively.

"I didn't mean that—"

"You don't have to apologize," she reassured him. "I jumped the gun. I can see that you trust me to get the job done."

"You did great work yesterday. I believe you'll do the same today," he stated, looking over his screen. "How long before your shift?"

"An hour and a half." She issued a sharp sigh. "I should get up and make something to eat."

"On it," he said, setting down his laptop and heading toward the kitchen.

"You're spoiling me," she teased in an attempt to lighten the tension from a few seconds ago when she'd overreacted.

"Anything for my new bride," he quipped in a surprising show of his sense of humor. It had peeked out a few times and she liked that side of him.

"Be careful. I can get used to this," she shot right back, enjoying the lightness of the conversation, realizing her day would end up another whirlwind. It might take a couple of days, but she would eventually get into a groove and, hopefully, the video footage would reveal something soon. Give them a path to follow.

"We should have something back about the sheriff before you head to work. Since I need to avoid the restaurant today, I might go into town and do a little grocery shopping. Check out the local scene," he said as amazing smells emanated from the kitchen.

"What are you cooking?" she asked.

"Eggs," he said. "I called your older brother Shane last night while you were at work and he said you love scrambled eggs, toast and jam for breakfast."

"Wait a minute. How did you get my brother's number?" she asked. "And how do you know his name?"

Quint shrugged his broad shoulders. She forced her gaze away from his muscled back.

"You need to tell me before I get really angry," she said.

"Technically, he called me," he confessed.

"He wouldn't do that," she said. Would he?

On second thought, that was exactly what her older brother would do. As the oldest, Shane had always felt responsible for his siblings. "Was he worried he gave me bad advice?"

"It sounded like he was. He seemed bothered by the fact the two of you didn't have a chance to talk the situation through," he said.

"How did he get your number?" she asked.

"Through the department, but he requested that I not tell you. He said he was afraid you might come on too strong after the two of you spoke on the phone. Everything happened so fast, he said, and then you cut off the conversation," Quint said.

"If he asked you not to tell me, then why are you?" she asked, curious as to why he would break her brother's trust.

"If we're going to be 'married' we can't have any division between us. No secrets. I thanked your brother for touching base with me and saw how much he cared about you. But I told him I couldn't go behind your back. I didn't tell you last night because we got off topic and you needed rest. I'm telling you now because this was the earliest point that I could bring it up," he said, turning to study her like he was gauging her reaction.

"Sounds like my big brother," she said with a sigh. "Always looking out for me."

Quint set the plate down on the two-top in the kitchen area. "Breakfast is served."

She cocked an eyebrow at him. "Did you make me my favorite breakfast to smooth over the fact you quizzed my brother about me last night?"

"I don't know," he said, feigning being offended. "Would it work?"

More than she wanted to admit. Ree shook her head and smiled.

QUINT WASN'T TRYING to roll her brother under the bus. He also didn't want to hide anything from her. It could show on his face at a critical moment. There could be no secrets between them, especially one like this. He wasn't kidding about that before.

Ree crossed the room, coffee cup in hand. Lounge pants, a T-shirt and robe shouldn't be this sexy on a person. Her sleepy smile tugged at his heart as he pulled her chair back like a server might at a five-star restaurant.

She took a seat and he pushed it in, handing over a napkin.

"If this is what waking up is like, I'll take this treatment every day," she said with a smile that smacked him square in the chest.

"You should be treated like an angel," he said so low he wasn't sure she heard him. Did he want her to?

Good question, he thought, trying to convince himself that he was only stoking the flame of attraction to "sell" their relationship to others when they were in public. He was doing nothing more than method acting. An annoying little voice in the back of his mind said there was more to it, but he wasn't ready to unpack the meaning just yet.

"Are you eating with me?" she asked.

"I'm not missing out on scrambled eggs and toast," he said, appreciating the lightness happening between them. It was a good way to bond and build a partnership—a partnership that could mean the difference between life and death. He needed to work with a sketch artist today while the bald guy and the one with the ruddy complexion were fresh on his mind. He could accomplish that while Ree worked, too.

As he walked over to the stove and plated his food, he flashed back to all the times he'd made breakfast for Tessa. Bagels, cream cheese and jam had been her hands-down favorite. Coffee with milk and two raw sugars had been her go-to before the pregnancy. He'd missed another sign early on because she'd switched over to decaf. Tessa had most definitely never been a decaf person. The only reason he'd caught on to the change was because he surprised her with one of her favorite coffeehouse drinks only to realize she let it sit on her desk. Before, the vanilla mocha would be gone in a heartbeat.

The memories fell into the category of too late and of no use anymore. He set his plate down on the table so hard there was a noise and eggs got shuffled around on the plate.

Ree gasped. Her gaze darted toward him before dropping to his hand where he fisted his fork. Quint released his grip and the fork tumbled onto the table.

He sat down without making eye contact.

"Anything you want to talk about?" Ree asked, pushing a clump of egg around with her fork.

"No," he said with a finality that should tell her this subject was off-limits. He needed to find a way to get through this assignment without thinking about Tessa every hour. No matter how hard he tried, his mind kept cycling back to how he'd failed her when she'd needed him most.

Ree took in a slow breath that he could hear from across the table. And then another. She didn't immediately move. She didn't speak. She seemed to realize this wasn't the time for words. He wouldn't be able to find the right ones to express his anger, frustration and disappointment at himself anyway. Instead, the two of them sat in the same companionable silence and suddenly Quint felt an intimacy and connection to someone like he'd never known through spoken words.

He couldn't be certain how long they stayed at the table but at some point he picked up his fork and began eating. Ree finished her plate, gathered both once they were empty, and then disappeared into the bathroom.

A short time later, she came back out, kissed him on the cheek and said, "Any word yet about the sheriff? I'm leaving for work now."

"I can check if you have a minute," he said.

She glanced at her cell. "I'd better not hang around. It'll look good if I'm a few minutes early to work and I might be able to strike up a conversation with one of the other waitresses in the breakroom."

"I'd like to walk you over, at least. It'll familiarize Charley with me. Plus, he'll see that I'm respecting his boundary by stopping at the door." He instinctively reached for her hand, then stood when he found it.

"Okay." Her smile was sunshine after a monsoon. "I'd like that a lot actually."

Ree led the way. He left the cabin door unlocked during the short walk. He stopped at the restaurant door and planted a kiss on his "wife" that caused a tornado of heat to swirl in his chest. When they pulled apart, both were breathless. They opened their eyes at the same time and he saw a deep well of need in her glittery green eyes.

All he could think was...*damn*.

There hadn't been anyone so off-limits and so tempting that he could ever remember. The breakup in his twenties seemed like nothing compared to what would happen if it was Ree instead of Maisy.

For a long moment, he stood at the door after she walked inside. Then he pulled it together and headed home. Halfway across the parking lot he realized he didn't have on his boot. Quint cursed. It wasn't like him to slip and that was a huge one as far as errors went. He could only pray the mistake wouldn't cause unwanted attention or harm the investigation in any way. He cursed again.

As he rounded the corner to the cabin, he saw the unlocked door was open.

Quint glanced around, surveying the area. This cabin was closest to the restaurant and had the least amount of privacy from the road. He took in a deep breath, calming his racing pulse. Going in looking like an officer would risk blowing their cover. After Bald Guy and Ruddy Complexion last night and the fact Ree's cover might have been compromised, Quint's radar was on high alert. Was someone on to them?

Chapter Seven

Back flat against the building, Quint eased toward the opened door. He peeked inside. It took a second for his gaze to adjust to the dark cabin after walking in the bright Texas sun.

No one was in sight in the open living space, but he heard the sound of the hallway door being opened. The washer opened and closed. Then, the dryer. Someone was rooting around in their cabin. Did Charley catch on? Bald Guy? Ruddy Complexion?

With light steps, Quint moved into the main living room. He reached for his ankle holster, and then retrieved his SIG Sauer. Whoever was snooping around was moving through in a hurry. The medicine cabinet in the bathroom opened next.

Quint checked his laptop and saw an unfamiliar thumb drive. There were protocols in place to block any attempt to steal information. But he didn't like this one bit.

Keeping his attention on the bathroom, he moved over to his laptop and pocketed the memory stick.

As he moved to the mouth of the hallway, an older woman stepped out of the bathroom.

She let out a yelp as she clutched her heart. "Sorry. You scared me."

She was short, five feet two inches if he had to guess. She had a round middle, timeworn skin and gray eyes. Her hair was piled on top of her head and she looked like the kind of person who would always have candy tucked inside her apron pocket. Not exactly what he expected to come across and definitely not a skilled thief, but she could have been paid to snoop. Based on her reaction, he figured that was the case.

"My wife and I will be staying here for a long time," he started, playing the part of a newlywed and hoping she didn't see the boot he should be wearing that was propped up against the chair in the living room or the weapon he hid behind his leg. If she just got there, he should be fine. "There's no need for cleaning this cabin during our stay."

"I thought this cabin was going to turn over today. Let me see." She put on reading glasses that were on a string around her neck and then pulled a small notepad out of her pocket. Her hands were empty save for her cell. She didn't appear to have taken anything, so she might have been snapping pics. "This is number eight, right?"

"Number three." He took a couple of steps back and then pointed to the open front door, and the number on it.

"Oh, really?" She seemed genuinely shocked,

which meant she was a good actress. "I'm new. I must have read the number wrong. Serves me right for not putting on my glasses. I'll just get out of your way." She started scurrying around, gathering the supplies she'd set out on the kitchen counter.

"No rush." He walked over to the chair and sat down. Without being obvious, he scooted the boot out of her sight and out of the line of sight of the door.

While she was distracted, he slipped off his walking boot and tucked his foot inside the apparatus.

"Please don't tell the office about the mix-up, sir." She spun around as he reached for his laptop.

"Honest mistake," he said with a shrug and a smile. "They won't hear it from me."

"Thank you, sir." Her face dropped for just a second when she glanced at the spot where the thumb drive had been.

"Do you mind locking the door on your way out?" he asked, motioning toward his foot, making certain she noted he was injured.

"Oh, no, not at all. I don't mind at all," she stammered as she moved toward the door like a swirling dust cloud. She peeked her head back in before closing the door. "Thank you for understanding, sir."

"Not a problem," he said. "We all make mistakes. You barely set foot inside here. No harm, no foul."

"You're very kind," she said.

"I didn't catch your name," he said.

"Patricia," she said before closing the door and getting out of there as fast as she could.

The snick of a lock came a few seconds later.

Quint bolted toward the window and watched as the older woman waddled away. Then, just to be one hundred percent certain, he swept the place for bugs.

Once he was assured the cabin was clear, he retrieved his cell phone and called Agent Grappell, who picked up on the first ring.

"I walked in on a cleaning lady in the cabin who was going through our stuff," Quint said after perfunctory greetings. "She tried to use a thumb drive on my laptop."

"Give me a description and a name," Grappell said, as the click-click of his fingers on a keyboard came through the line.

"All I got out of her was *Patricia*," Quint said. He made a fresh cup of coffee before returning to his chair. "She exited darn fast once I caught her in the act."

He sent over pictures of several license plates from last night. He'd homed in on lone male drivers. He kept a couple of photos of the parking lot when it was full, for a comparison. In his experience, repeat customers tended to park in the same spot every time if it was available. People who were comfortable at a place had a tendency to repeat their patterns, including ordering the same meal.

Give him a week and he'd have better data. One night wouldn't be enough unless he got lucky, in which case he needed to use that luck to buy a lottery ticket. The front and side parking lots were interesting, but he planned to target most of his attention on what happened in back. The liquor truck from last night interested him, but in his experience criminals weren't usually so obvious. At least, not the good ones. Those would use a meat supplier truck or dairy. Something people wouldn't think twice about if they were pulled alongside it on the roadway, not giving it a second glance.

"I'll do a little digging," Grappell said. "See what I can come up with."

"My gut feeling is someone paid her to do it," he stated. "She was an amateur."

Quint went on to explain the pair from the bar last night. "I'd like to work with Aaron to come up with a sketch of these two if he's available. Run it past Lionel to see if we can get anything out of him."

More clicks came through the line.

"I'll have Aaron call," Grappell said. "Lionel has gotten quiet on us."

"He's scared," Quint said. "Romanian gangs are lethal, and they have long fingers."

"Which is why the boss has requested he be placed in the infirmary until this case is over," Grappell said. "He'll get twenty-four-hour security there."

"We might get more out of him that way," Quint agreed. He also realized this case had bigger implications if the boss employed a tactic like that. "How do you want the thumb drive?"

"Any chance you can overnight it?" Grappell said. "It's too dangerous to risk a drop."

"I can do that. I'm driving into town today anyway under the guise of running errands and meeting people," he said. "It's probably too late to get a print. Patricia had on plastic cleaning gloves."

"Convenient," Grappell said.

"Isn't it," Quint stated, thinking the same thing.

"We'll dust anyway, see what we can find," Grappell said. "I'll run employment records with the rental agency for the cabin to see if we come up with a match."

"Good." Quint figured it couldn't hurt. "What did you find out about Sheriff Rice?"

"I sent an email half an hour ago, but there haven't been any investigations or blemishes. His record is clean so far."

"Maybe he's a good guy after all," Quint said before ending the call. Charley could be the bad seed, running weapons right underneath the nose of his squeaky-clean cousin. *Interesting.* Wouldn't be the first time Quint had witnessed a similar scenario. This news, in many ways, made his and Ree's job easier. Dirty law enforcement officers had been rare in his professional career and the few he'd come across infuriated him. They were usually hard to catch and deadly if they figured an agent out. There was no worse crime than someone who'd sworn to uphold the law turning on the people he or she was supposed to protect.

He had no patience for people who made it harder to do his job or caused the public to lose respect for his profession—a profession he loved even if he could admit the job was losing some of its spark lately. But then, since losing Tessa, he could say the same thing about life.

Rather than go down that path again, he decided to get out of the cabin and do a little digging around in town. In his experience, investigations only took one spark to get off the ground. Quint wanted to get a sense of Charley's reputation while in town.

He also wanted to stop at the hardware store and buy a new lock.

GOING IN EARLY had been a bust. The second day of work was much like the first, a whirlwind. Lunch came and went in a blur. Ree's feet felt like they might literally fall off by the time the dinner rush started. She'd failed miserably at getting to know the kitchen staff so far, and the earlier text from Preston was a distraction she couldn't afford while she was undercover.

The band was setting up over in one corner of the bar on a small triangle-shaped stage. Ree was busy with her station when she noticed a couple of waitresses she hadn't met yet coming in through the back door.

"Do the white-boot waitresses only work the bar? No food shifts?" Ree looked to Adrian, who rolled her eyes.

"Those are the barmaids," Adrian said. She motioned toward her chest area. "Notice a difference between them and us?"

Before Ree could respond, Adrian added, "Well, maybe not you but definitely me and Zoey. There are a couple other waitresses you haven't met yet who work the dining room and they look more like me in that department."

"Come on, you're beautiful," Ree pointed out.

"I do all right," Adrian said, swatting her hand at Ree. "But those barmaids are stacked." Adrian made eyes at Ree and Ree laughed. "You could be one of them, but you have to work here for at least six months before you can even be considered. Then I hear Charley is the one who asks."

"Sounds like the A-team," Ree said before realizing she might have insulted Adrian. "Not that you aren't."

"I've only been here four months and Zoey has been here a month less than me," Adrian said on a shrug. "Neither of us have put in enough time but I can only imagine the tips they make. They work Thursday through Sunday night, when the bar picks up."

"We do all right," Ree stated. "I've never made more money working at a restaurant."

The best way to describe the trio of waitresses was *extra*. Their lashes had to be fake. Good, but fake. There was no way natural lashes were long enough to see from this distance. Their uniforms had sparkles on them and their white boots had been polished and spit shined. Ree glanced down at her shirt that was in okay shape. She probably should have ironed it after it came out of the dryer. Her brown boots were her own but they didn't nearly stand out in the way the trio's white ones did.

No one on the dining room floor had on expensive boots.

Ree figured there was no way she was going to be here long enough to make six months on the job. She would never be part of the special group of waitresses and it might not be a big deal. Could she befriend one? Get information? Looking at the way they sashayed their hips after they high-fived and started toward the dining area, Ree wondered if all they did was waitress. Grappell had run a list of names of the staff. It appeared to be outdated considering the head count on waitresses was off, but then there was probably a lot of turnover in this industry. She needed to put her head together with Quint and figure out if these ladies were paid under the table. It would be an easy way to hide a person.

"Good job today, Red," Chef shouted from behind the counter dividing his space and hers.

"Thank you," she said, realizing this was the first time he'd complimented her.

"Fender should have a good report for the boss." Chef was short, in his late forties, with thick wiry hair that was slicked back and graying at the temples.

"That's a relief," she said. Fender and Charley met at the end of the shift outside in the back while Fender had a cigarette. With the meeting being held behind the restaurant, there was no guarantee the two only discussed work. Ree had been told they discussed the waitstaff, but they could be talking about any number of things. Speaking of which, Charley's cousin was in the bar tonight having a social drink with one of his deputies. It would be nice if Quint was here, too, but being overly eager could cast suspicion and that would defeat the whole purpose.

She also wished she could stick around and have a drink so she could get to know the barmaids better, but Charley had been clear about leaving when her shift was done. She'd put in a food order for her "injured" husband a few minutes ago, figuring it would give her an excuse to hang around a bit after her shift.

"My husband got hurt on the job and I need this job while he finishes his certification," she continued, picking up the conversation thread with Chef.

"Oh yeah? Sorry to hear it. What did your husband use to do?" Chef asked, leaning toward her. Another sign he was interested in what she had to say.

She realized a few ears had perked up near where they were standing. No one looked over at them and she figured Chef had all their respect.

"Owned a moving company," she said. "He stopped by yesterday. Sat over there." She motioned toward the counter.

"Oh, right. I remember him. Big guy," he said. "Wore a boot."

"That's the one." She had no idea where this conversation was going. Interesting to note that Chef remembered Quint. Although, to be fair, his stature and good looks made an impression. She didn't want to think about how convenient his physical attributes were when trying to get information from the opposite sex.

"What happened to him? If you don't mind my

asking," Chef continued, grabbing the towel off his shoulder before wetting it in the sink.

"I don't." She shrugged. "He hit it on a curb while carrying a piano. It came down hard, he landed funny, and shattered his ankle. We got sued and that's when we found out the partner handling the books let our liability insurance lapse. Basically, we lost everything and that was a month into our marriage. So, here we are."

She threw her hands in the air, praying that she hadn't just given too much detail, the hallmark of a lie.

Chef winced at the part about the piano going down on Quint's ankle and she figured that was a good sign her story was believable. She needed to update Quint so he wasn't caught off guard with any of these details the next time he showed up here.

"That's too bad," he said, squirting cleaner on the metal prep surface before wiping with the wet towel.

"He's learning how to program computers now, though," she said.

"A desk job." Chef put a hand on his lower back and stretched. "Can't work on your feet for ten to twelve hours a day forever without breaking your back."

"I just hope he can do it," she admitted. "He's used to being active all day. But he says he's not twenty any longer."

"Amen to that," Chef agreed.

"He always liked tinkering around with computers.

Said he might as well figure out how to work 'em," she said.

"When he does, maybe he can take a look at the one I have at home." Chef shook his head. "It stopped turning on last week and I have my life on that thing. Can't even pay my bills in two weeks if I can't get it up and running." He put his hands up, wrists together. "It's got me handcuffed."

"I won't make any promises but Quint sure could use the practice," she said, figuring this was a start to gaining her coworker's trust.

"Maybe you could give me his number and I could give him a call," he said.

"Absolutely," she said. "Let me go get my cell. I haven't memorized anyone's number since high school, not even my husband's."

Chef laughed. "I don't know my own mother's number. I just push the contact and, bam, there she is on the line."

"Same." Ree disappeared into the breakroom, grabbed her purse and returned.

Chef stood on her side of the counter with a to-go bag in one hand and his cell in the other. "Dinner is ready. I threw in a few extra rolls and doubled the portion. You barely ate your dinner."

"Thank you. That's really kind of you," she said, holding her phone out with Quint's information.

"I'll give him a call tomorrow," Chef said.

"I hope he can figure it out. The practice sure will be good for him." She hoped this wasn't getting too off track with the investigation. Chef seemed about as honest and hardworking as they came. But then, this job had taught her looks could be deceiving, and everyone was a suspect until ruled out based on fact.

She held up the bag. "Thanks again for this."

Chef nodded but his warm smile touched her. Was it wrong to wish he wasn't involved? It wouldn't change her investigation but she would be disappointed in humanity if he was implicated.

What better cover for an operation than to have genuinely good people in place and a cousin for a sheriff? Ree had a lot to share with Quint and couldn't wait to get home to talk to him.

Chapter Eight

Quint stood outside the restaurant, boot on, waiting for his "wife." He did his level best not to be obvious about checking out the bar scene. The music thumped and it sounded lively in there. He tapped the toe of his good foot to the beat, noticing additional head count.

Ree came into view and his heart fisted. She stepped outside and met his gaze. Time stilled. All he could hear was a whoosh sound in his ears as blood rushed through his body. This was the same effect of an adrenaline rush without the smoking gun aimed at his chest.

Admittedly, he'd thought about Ree more times than he could count today, and spent even more time telling himself it was necessary for the investigation. The annoying voice in the back of his head countered his argument every time.

Right now, though, all he wanted to do was hold her against him and kiss those pink lips of hers. The kiss was for show, so he decided to be convincing.

By the time their lips parted, they were both left gasping for air, chests heaving. If anyone watched, they should be convinced the two of them were into each other. Thankfully, he didn't have to fake an attraction to her.

"Sorry about that," he said low and under his breath, still in the mental fog that was Ree.

"About what?" she asked, slowly opening her eyes.

"All the kissing," he said, remembering the stance she'd taken yesterday.

"If it has to be done," she said, still a little breathless. His ego didn't mind the fact she seemed to be just as affected as he was every time they were this close. She cleared her throat and put on a smile. "I mean…it's important. You know?"

"Yes, which probably makes it wrong that I'm enjoying it so much." There. He'd said it. He couldn't stop himself. Plus, it was true.

Ree rewarded him with a smile that could melt ice in a freezer.

"Something smells amazing," he said, redirecting the conversation by taking the doggie bag and then linking their fingers.

"Tonight's special, packed by Chef himself," she said. "Chicken and waffles."

"My mouth is already watering," he said. The restaurant portion of the business was legit and bustling, which could make it easy to hide illegal activity. There was a reason that crimes often occurred in busy places. Folks were distracted. There was lots of mental stimulation, sensory overload.

"Your mouth is very talented," she quipped. Her cheeks turned two shades of crimson and pride swelled in his chest. His pulse kicked up a few notches, too.

"That's good to hear. I was afraid being out of practice would show," he admitted, and then wished he could reel the admission back in. A real attraction was out of the question with a colleague, so he did his best to quash his reaction.

"If being in practice gets better..." she said, the words so low he barely heard them.

Not the time to reply, Quint. Hand in hand, they crossed the parking lot. At the cabin, he opened the door for her. Once inside, he set the food bag on the table.

"Why don't you take a load off?" he asked, nodding toward the table.

She toed off her boots and gave him a quick and dirty rundown of the day's events, starting with the waitress trio. He made a note to check the roster Grappell had provided. "An establishment like Greenlight has a lot of moving parts, so it shouldn't be too surprising there is specialized staff. We can double-check the roster but these things are usually out of date and fluid."

"I sure hope you actually know something about fixing computers," she said with a smile after updating him on Chef's request.

"I'm handy. It's kind of a hobby of mine and the

reason it works as cover," he admitted. "I like to know how things work."

"Makes sense you'd use that in our cover story then," she agreed.

He pulled out two plates and filled them with food. The garlic mashed potatoes smelled out of this world and there was just enough spinach on the side to make two meals. He grabbed a Coke from the fridge and poured it into a glass with ice.

"When you do decide to get married, your wife is going to be the luckiest woman on earth," Ree said as she seemed to take in the setup.

"Let's pretend that's not an option," he said, taking his seat. The first couple of bites sold him on Chef's cooking abilities. Hook. Line. And sinker.

"Why not?" She quirked a brow. "Think about ever getting married?"

"Not my particular brand of punishment," he stated.

"You wouldn't be so bad to live with," she shot back before quirking a smile. He could tell she grew up in a house of brothers, based on her sense of humor.

"Funny," he quipped, and she seemed content to leave the discussion alone. It was a closed subject as far as he was concerned.

"I've been serving this dish all night. I wasn't one hundred percent certain I could eat it if I wanted to but it's literally the best thing I've put in my mouth in ages," she said before blushing. "I mean, kissing you is pretty great, too."

"Well, thank you," he said, not minding the compliment.

"I just mean that you're pretty good at it. I can hardly tell you're acting at all," she said before taking a big bite of food, clearly oblivious to the hit he'd just taken to his pride.

Ouch. The offhand remark shouldn't bruise his ego like it did. No one had ever complained about his kissing abilities before. So why was he all of a sudden questioning himself? Rather than give away his true feelings, he laughed it off. "What can I say? I'm good like that."

"A little *too* good, if you ask me. But it's good for the investigation. You almost convinced me you meant it and I should know better." She shrugged as she chowed down, unaware of the fact she'd just delivered a second blow.

"It's good to put on a show in case someone's watching," he said.

"And someone is always watching while on a case," she quipped. "I know I'm new to the restaurant and, therefore, will be under scrutiny until I prove myself, but I can't help the feeling of being constantly watched."

"You're new. Might come with the territory," he said before updating her on Patricia.

"Do you think Bald Guy and Ruddy Complexion were behind the bribe?" she asked point-blank.

"No idea. But I did work with a sketch artist today on that subject." He grabbed his laptop and opened it to show her the sketches filling the screen.

"Those look good," she said, then pointed to Bald Guy. "He had a dark mole near the tip of his nose."

Quint took note.

"And Ruddy Complexion had thicker eyebrows." She examined the sketches for a long moment. "Other than that, these are on point."

Quint made the notations and sent an email to Aaron to make the changes.

"What did you find out in town?" she asked when she'd brought him up to speed on the rest of her day. Her plate was clean and her glass empty.

"Turns out Cricket Creek's Cricket Toss Festival used to use live crickets," he said with a forced smile.

"For real?" She scrunched her nose up and it only served to make her adorable.

"According to the lady who runs the post office, they stopped doing that years ago. Now all the critters are stuffed and no one gets hurt in the festivities." He polished off his meal and water glass in record time. The food at Greenlight was top-shelf. Of course, that could be part of the distraction. If folks showed up for the food and the live band, money flowed, and people had a good time. No one would dig too deep into the financials.

"At least they stopped. That's good," she said.

"You might want to hold off on your relief. They serve cricket pie and fried cricket," he said, unable to imagine a worse taste than either of those two.

Her entire body shook. "Oh, heck, no."

"Not exactly going to make the menu at Greenlight," he quipped.

"What else haven't we covered?" he asked, before remembering to give her the new key for the changed lock.

"I already know where you stand about marriage. Are you in a relationship?" she asked, catching him off guard with this line of questioning.

"Whoa there. I should have specified *work* questions," he said. "Ask away. While we check the footage from the past twenty-four hours."

He rinsed off the plates and then left them in the sink to be dealt with later. He slipped off his boot and brought his laptop over to the couch as he updated her on Lionel's situation.

"Do you mind if I grab a shower real quick? I need to wash the work ick off me," she said.

"Go for it. I'll go ahead and start." This was the tedious work of an investigation. Things didn't work in real life as they were portrayed on television. There was a whole lot of sorting through footage, gathering information, and then waiting. In life, cases weren't neatly wrapped up in less than an hour. He grabbed his laptop and checked the employee roster at Greenlight.

Quint heard the spigot being turned on in the room behind where he was sitting. An image of Ree slipping out of her clothes and into the water assaulted him. He gave himself a mental headshake, trying to erase the image. They didn't lack a spark between them but it was good she didn't seem attracted to him in a greater sense. Seriously. All good.

Running through the recording, Quint snapped a couple of screenshots. There were three repeat customers from yesterday. He opened a file and typed in the license plate numbers with a pic of each driver and their vehicles. He then sent the documents to Grappell. There was a dairy delivery around back that he took note of. Wednesday whiskey. Thursday dairy. Chef had come in both mornings by 7:00 a.m. with his arms full of bags of fresh ingredients. He made three trips to his sports car on Wednesday and five this morning, which probably coincided with anticipated business levels. Naturally, there'd be more customers on live band night. At least, that was the working assumption from his experience surveilling other restaurants.

Chef was in and out within an hour before returning three and a half hours later, presumably ahead of the lunch rush hit. No surprises there. Could the man pushing fifty be running weapons in those bags? Granted, looks could be deceiving, but Chef's short, apple-shaped body and hair that was graying at the temples made him come across as innocent. Despite the fact it didn't seem likely he was guilty, it was too early to cross anyone off the suspect list. Besides, trucks made the most sense in terms of moving the kind of volume that would have caught his agency's attention.

The sound of water shutting off behind him sent his thoughts back to the place they didn't need to go with Ree. Shoving them aside proved trickier than he'd have liked. He'd been distracted by her before and could have cost them their credibility. Quint refocused on the screen as he watched a guy go out back and have a smoke while he waited for someone. And that someone was Charley.

REE TOWELED OFF and dressed in her pajamas, thinking about how awkward she'd become with Quint after their kiss at the restaurant door. Seeing him standing there, waiting, had thrown her off-kilter. And then she'd tripped all over herself in conversation with the man.

She sighed. What could she do? Pick herself up and move on.

After brushing her teeth, she stood at the door ready to join him in the living area, doing her level best to forget how incredible his lips were when they were pressed against hers. And how right the world felt when she was in his arms. Ree had always relied on herself. Growing up with four brothers had toughened her up, taught her to depend on herself, and given her one wicked sense of humor. So the reaction she was having to Quint caught her off guard.

There was more heat when she was in the same room with him than during all of her past relationships combined. There was something a little unnerving about her attraction to him, an attraction there was no way he possibly reciprocated. He was going all in for show in order to sell them as a couple despite the bits of encouragement she'd received from him. It seemed he was trying to convince her, too. She took her hat off to the man. He was doing a great job of making her believe there might be something special brewing between them.

Ree could admit she'd been in a string of past relationships that didn't do much for her. Except Preston. He'd been different. She could blame her lack of interest in long-term dating on the focus on her career, but that wasn't exactly true. There hadn't been anyone who made her want more than a few dates or a casual fling. There hadn't been anyone who caused her heart to feel like it might explode out of her chest into a thousand flecks of dust if he walked out on her. And there hadn't been anyone who could kiss her so thoroughly that she was probably going to be ruined for every other man for life.

Another sigh and she was ready to face Quint. It was a short walk into the living room, so not a whole lot of time to rid herself of the aftershocks of her realizations. He sat there on the couch, barely glancing up at her as she entered the room. Rightly so. They weren't in public now and he could drop the facade.

He patted the seat next to him without looking up. "Want to see my notes so far?"

"Yes," she responded, hearing the frog sound in her own throat. She took the seat next to him and tucked her phone underneath her leg. Out of the corner of her eye, she saw him wrinkle his nose. It made her want to sniff herself to see if she had body odor but she'd just gotten out of the shower so that was impossible. He might not like her choice in bath products. She needed to get over it all because she'd never been one to get inside her own head about the lavender bodywash she used.

Quint pulled up a document and explained what he'd observed so far. He brought her up to speed on Chef's routine.

"Is it strange the barmaids come through the back door instead of the front?" she asked.

"It might be but I don't think it's unusual considering they enter while customers are already in-house dining. They probably don't want to parade them in front of the tables while people are still eating," he stated before picking up a small device from the coffee table. "This should help us figure out what's going on in the breakroom."

"Right. I meant to ask about a listening device," she said.

"I didn't want this to be anywhere near you for your first couple of days at Greenlight in case Charley or one of his cohorts suspected something might be up with you," he said. "I do think it's safe now, so you can drop it in the bottom of your handbag so it'll be on-site when you are."

"Of course, we don't have any evidence so far that would convince a judge to give us a warrant so we can listen in," she stated.

"Exactly. I'm planning to place a similar device out back but I need to make certain there are no cameras back there that might bust me. Have you seen anything that might indicate there are?" he asked.

"I haven't been out back yet," she said. Her gut

instinct said Charley was a smart character and he would take precautions.

Right now, she wanted to ignore the way her heart pounded in her chest when she breathed in Quint's spicy masculine scent and home in on finding answers.

Chapter Nine

Quint wrinkled his nose again as he breathed in Ree's fresh-from-the-shower, lavender scent. She had an effect on him like no one else. Was his attraction to Ree inconvenient? Yes. Was it getting in the way of his better judgment? If he thought so, he needed to pull himself from this case immediately. The only question that mattered was whether or not he could contain it and continue in a professional manner, because when her mouth was moving against his, all logic flew out the window and he was engulfed in a flame that threatened to turn into a raging wildfire.

He pulled up the document for Ree, noticing the excitement in her voice. Was she on to something?

She inched a little closer as she studied the screen like it was finals week in college. Her tongue darted across her bottom lip, and he tried to ignore the silky trail it left.

"What is it, Ree?"

"Phillip." She pointed toward a blond-haired guy from truck number two. "I'm almost a hundred percent sure I overheard Adrian call him by this name at some point."

Quint took down the information, placing a question mark next to the name.

"He must be a regular if Adrian knows him," she said. "I wish there was a break in between shifts so I could really talk to her. You know, ask for the lay of the land. Find out who is who and some background information on everyone. But that would be difficult to do without sounding like an investigator."

"True. If we're too eager or ask too many questions it could put the spotlight on us," he said, realizing he had to be more careful after the boot incident. It wasn't like him to be sloppy and he sure hoped he was able to cover, but he didn't like making mistakes. She nodded. "We might be in this one for a few weeks, a month." He glanced at her. "Or it could be done in four days. My experience has been all over the map."

"Somehow, I don't think this one will be like that," she said. "But if we're going to be a couple for longer than a few days, we should probably dig a little deeper into each other's lives."

He didn't mind sharing a little bit about his background for the sake of the investigation. Plus, a surprising part of him wanted to talk to her about Tessa.

"Do you know about my former partner?" Quint asked on a sharp sigh, figuring he needed to get that part of his history out of the way. He might have a desire to share but that didn't mean it was going to be easy.

"I think I heard something," she admitted.

"Do you know what happened to her?" he asked.

"I can piece bits of the story together, but I'd like to hear your version," she said, taking in a slow breath.

"She was killed in the line of duty when we were working with another agency," he said. "You know how it is. We don't always have time to get to know each other or rehearse before it's go time."

"Those little things like who likes to come in from the right get glossed over," she said. "It's one of the easiest ways to be killed on the job."

She did know and it sounded like she had a story to tell. Had her father's high-speed crash resulted from another agency getting involved?

"Tessa." He flashed eyes at Ree. "That was her name. Tessa was more than my partner."

Ree's gaze widened and he realized the implication.

"She was my best friend," he quickly added.

"Were you in love?" she asked before seeming like she tried to quickly reel the question back in.

"I loved her but not in the romantic sense," he admitted. "We had a long history and were basically the same person on the inside."

"Did you ever date?" she asked.

"No, because I think we always knew we were too much alike to be anything more than friends," he said. "Plus, it was much more like brother and sister. I'm sure you can relate to the thought of dating one of your brothers being less than appealing."

The puckered face she made proved it. She faux-gagged in a way that was both endearing and funny.

"That's basically the way I felt about Tessa. I will always love her but dating was always out of the question for both of us. She was pretty but I was never attracted to her in the same way that…" Had he really just almost admitted to an attraction to Ree? "Suffice it to say that we never even tried to go there with each other. We bonded over similar upbringings and had a lot in common, not the least of which was going into law enforcement. We both had someone step in during a critical time in our lives whom we credit with saving us."

"Parallel lives?" she asked.

"You could say that," he said. "Except that she got into a relationship that ended with a pregnancy."

"Ended?"

"The guy bolted the minute he found out Tessa was carrying his child. Said it couldn't be his and accused her of cheating on the relationship." Quint fisted his hands. He flexed and released his fingers a couple of times to work off some of the tension of talking about it. Tessa being treated badly was a sore subject with him.

Ree surprised him by reaching over and touching his hands. "He sounds like a real jerk. Why is it that smart, beautiful women can walk into the trap of falling for a creep?"

Her words were balm to soothe a wounded soul. She brought more of that light to the darkest corners inside his soul.

"This guy doesn't want to ever run into me in a dark alley," he said, realizing that was probably the wrong answer and not caring. Five minutes alone with Mr. Jerk and the guy would think twice about getting a woman pregnant and then accusing her of sleeping around to get out of his responsibilities. Of course, Tessa could have forced a paternity test once the kid was born and gotten child support at the very least. But she hadn't wanted anything to do with a man who could walk away from his own flesh and blood like that. Based on personal experience with his own non-dad, Quint couldn't agree more.

"Or me," Ree added, as indignant as he was. "Or any one of my brothers."

"Sounds like you had the family we all wished for," he said.

"We have our problems and disagreements, believe me, but we love each other to the moon and back," she said. The warmth in her eyes poured more light into the dark.

He'd read as much in Shane's voice during their phone call.

Ree was studying him when he brought his gaze up to meet hers. "What aren't you telling me about the situation?" she asked quietly.

THERE WAS A storm brewing behind Quint's eyes, a storm she recognized from the conversation they'd had at the table right before he'd shut down and walked away earlier.

"About Tessa?" he asked, and she could tell from his tone that he was holding something back.

"Or the situation in general," she clarified. "What exactly happened on the bust?"

"Other than the fact she died?" he asked, his cold words cutting a hole in her chest. He seemed to regret his word choice immediately when he added, "It's all still a little raw and I'm a whole lot of angry. I didn't mean for that to come out the way it sounded or be so blunt."

"You know what? You don't have to apologize to me for being human," she said. Growing up around guys had made her able to read through the lines when something was aimed at her or the world. Quint's anger fell into the latter camp.

He didn't speak for a long moment. But when he did, he said, "Thank you. I can't say that anyone has understood what I meant rather than what I said before. I'm generally the king of miscommunication in relationships."

"You're welcome, Quint. Here's the thing. We might be here for two more days or two months. Neither of us ever really knows what the future is going to bring, especially on a case. So, if we can really talk and do a little good here between us, it'll make the time in between following up on leads or general investigating a whole lot more meaningful." Ree surprised herself with the realization even though she meant every word. Truths like this came from the heart and she couldn't have scripted it any better to get her point across.

Quint rocked his head.

"You're right," he said. "I just don't normally talk to people."

"Ever?"

He shook his head. "Not since Tessa."

"I'd like to be friends, Quint." This whole attraction welling up inside her, gaining steam, wished for something else, something more. But she would settle for friendship.

"She shouldn't have died," he confessed. Saying the words out loud seemed to take a lot of energy. "It was my fault."

"I can't imagine that to be true," she said.

"What makes you say that?" he asked.

"Because you aren't the kind of person who would go back on an assignment if you had been responsible for someone's death. You would punish yourself for years to come and I highly doubt you'd ever do the same job again," she said.

He nodded.

"The reason it's my fault is because I let her convince me to keep quiet about the pregnancy when she should have been on desk duty. Now my godchild is…"

The news Quint was to be a godfather to Tessa's baby caused a half dozen puzzle pieces to click together about the strength of their bond and the amount of guilt he must be feeling for letting Tessa down, like he believed he had.

Ree highly doubted Tessa would blame Quint for keeping her secret, but the blow that would cause to a person like Quint would devastate most others. The burden he'd been carrying around with him at the double blow would crush a lesser human.

"I'm so sorry," she whispered as she leaned into him. She had no idea, at that point, if her touch was welcome or not but it was all she had to give in the way of comfort. There was no way in hell she could sit idly by and watch him suffer if there was anything she could do about it.

He wrapped his arms around her, so she scooted closer. The steady rhythm of his heartbeat against her body comforted her beyond words and she could only hope he felt half the same as her in that moment.

"It's not your fault," she said quietly, reassuringly.

"Yeah?" he asked and she could hear his voice break. "Because it sure as hell feels like it is exactly my fault. I had the power to stop her from doing something that caused her to die. I should have been the one to force the desk duty issue sooner so she would still be here, dammit."

There was so much pain and anguish in his voice that her heart nearly cracked in half.

"I know you feel that way and I know it feels like the truth right now. But you would never have done anything to hurt Tessa or her baby," she said in as calm a voice as she could muster. She drew on all the compassion she had when she added, "Other people's choices are not your fault. You did what she asked because you trusted her to make the right decisions."

"I shouldn't have and then she would still be here holding her daughter in her arms instead of…" His distress was palpable.

The sound of beer bottles being slammed against a wall broke into the heavy moment. Quint kicked into gear as immediately as Ree did.

"Boot," she reminded as it seemed to dawn on him, too.

He bolted toward it, taking the extra few seconds to strap it on as she flew to the window, listening.

"Two male voices," she whispered before risking a peek. "Charley just came running out the front door with Phillip." She paused a couple of seconds to watch as Quint took off toward the front door. "Oh, goodness."

"What's going on?" Quint's fingers were already wrapped around the door handle.

"They're arguing," she said.

"Is it possible Phillip's drunk?" he asked, pausing at the door.

"From here it looks so. I'll ask about it tomorrow at work and see if I can get anything else. It'll make a nice conversation starter with Adrian," she said as Quint backed away from the door.

"It's getting late and you need rest if you're going back there for the whole day again," he finally said. "I'll grab a shower."

"Quint?" she began.

"Yeah?" He stopped halfway across the room but didn't turn to look at her.

"Thank you for trusting me earlier," she said. "It means more than you could ever know."

"It's a two-way street," he said quietly. There was a stillness to his voice that brought her nerves down a few notches after the excitement. "And I'd appreciate if you kept everything I've said between us."

"I wouldn't tell a soul," she said, hearing the defensiveness in her own voice. Rather than apologize for it, she left it out there.

"There's more to it but that's as far as I can go with it tonight," he said. There was a detached quality to his tone now. So she shifted her focus to Charley and Phillip and the buzz of questions she anticipated at the beginning of tomorrow's shift.

Chapter Ten

Ree arrived fifteen minutes early to work the next day. The minute she walked into the kitchen, Chef greeted her.

"I just called your husband," he said, looking mighty proud of himself. "He sounds like a good guy."

"I'd like to think so," she said with a friendly wink.

The gesture seemed to endear her to the older man's heart.

"He's coming over after I set up for the lunch rush to take a look at my machine," Chef said.

"Thanks for giving him the chance," she said. After the way she and Quint left things last night, it was hard to rally the fun-loving newlywed act. Her heart went out to him for what he'd been through and she wished there was something she could do to ease his pain.

"Here's hoping he can fix the problem," Chef hoisted his glass of water in the air in a mock toast.

"Yep," she said, remembering the listening device she had stashed at the bottom of her purse. She held up her handbag. "I better put this thing away and get ready for my shift."

"Hope the tips are good today," Chef said.

She really hoped he wasn't involved in any way because Chef had wormed his way inside her heart. She also realized she couldn't afford to let anyone but Quint in. It was too risky because she could miss a critical piece of evidence if she had blinders on. And then there was the simple fact that some people who seemed amazing on the outside were hardened criminals. Some people had an ability to compartmentalize their lives like nobody's business.

"I'll be right back," she said, leaving him to put away her handbag. She hoped to get a little more insight into conversations among kitchen staff later. Pele and Craig kept to themselves, and Eddie only ever nodded and smiled. When her shift started rocking and rolling, it would be game time and she barely had a chance to breathe, let alone gain valuable intel. She needed to feel Adrian and Zoey out to see if they were on to her after the Sarah and Marcus debacle. Of course, she realized Quint was working hard behind the scenes. She also figured him getting into Chef's computer was a huge win. At the very least, they might be able to rule him out as a suspect.

Ree walked out of the breakroom to find Chef almost exactly where she'd left him a minute ago. "So, did you hear about what happened last night?"

Chef shook his head. He walked a small square and then said, "This is my domain. What happens outside this area is none of my business."

"Smart," she said, figuring he was loyal to Charley at the very least.

He leaned over the metal counter. "I'll tell you what, though. A guy has been giving Charley a hard time lately. This is the third time this person has shown up in the past few days." Chef threw his hands in the air. "Something about money owed but it must be personal. The guy isn't one of our vendors to my knowledge."

Adrian bolted in last minute, looking in a frenzy and breaking into the conversation.

"Has Charley been around today?" she asked as she scurried past.

"I haven't seen him yet," Ree said, before giving Chef a smile and exiting the kitchen.

Zoey was on her side of the room, checking bottles and saltshaker lids. She didn't speak a whole lot and definitely not to Ree. She figured this might be a good time to strike up a conversation and get a feel for Zoey and her situation. If Adrian's suspicion was correct that Zoey was in some type of trouble, Ree had to intervene before she moved on from the investigation.

"Hey, did you hear what happened around here last night?" Ree asked.

Zoey didn't turn around. "No."

"It was a drunk guy," she continued. "I think his name is Phillip. Do you know him?"

Zoey shrugged. She wasn't much more than skin and bones despite a beautiful face.

The glass door opened.

"Looks like we have our first customer," Ree said to Zoey, trying to build some comradery.

Zoey turned to the side and nodded. There was a fresh-looking bruise on her forearm that she was trying to cover with makeup. Granted, Ree could attest to the bumps and bruises that came with this job, but her warning bells sounded nonetheless.

Holding her tongue for now, Ree headed back to her own station as Adrian returned to the room.

"What a day," Adrian said, wiping down her shirt that was markedly wrinkled. "And it hasn't even gotten started yet."

Adrian rolled her eyes as Zoey took the first customer to her own station.

"What's wrong with her?" Ree asked, feigning frustration.

Adrian shrugged as the second customer came in. "I try not to get too involved. You know what I mean? Everyone has to do their own thing and it's best not to ask too many questions."

"So true," Ree agreed despite this going against everything she believed in and was trained to do. Helping others was embedded in her DNA. "I shouldn't stick my nose where it doesn't belong."

"Especially not around here," Adrian said before seeming to catch herself. She glanced around before retying her blouse. Did she know something? She had to.

Thankfully, more customers started filing in and the rest of Ree's shift became a blur. She was more than ready to get home and put her feet up after cashing out her last table.

The car was gone, as was Quint. A note on the fridge read: *Out helping Chef. Be back soon. Lunch is in the fridge. Love, Q.*

Ree spent her break cleaning her boots and munching down on the sandwich he'd made for her. As much as she loved to rely on nobody but herself, it was nice to be able to lean on someone else for a change. It was a foreign thought to her that she could maintain her independence and still draw strength from someone. Funny to think this hadn't occurred to her before age thirty-six.

When this investigation was over, she had a lot to chew on with regard to her views on relationships. There really had only been one person in her past she could see herself dating long-term. Preston. Had she been too hasty to cut off their relationship after their last fling? The old cliché about absence making the heart grow fonder made her wonder if that was the case here. Because she was starting to miss Preston. Or maybe it was just being in a relationship that she missed. Dating her brother's best friend came with complications. The downside had been Shane knowing too much about her personal life. With four brothers, going out with someone who didn't know her family or wasn't friends with one of them had proved difficult enough. When she'd been in school, there wasn't really a way out of it. Now that she was grown, however, she'd made a promise to separate her dating life from family. There'd been too many times when one of her brothers had intervened on behalf of a friend.

Did she want to deal with that for the rest of her life? And why did her mind snap to wishing she could find a man like Quint out in the real world?

QUINT PULLED UP in front of the cottage-style house in town off Main Street. From the outside, Chef's place could best be described as tidy. There were window boxes filled with fresh flowers and the yard was nicely manicured.

A bright yellow sports car roared up behind Quint. The man Ree had described as Chef came out of the driver's seat. He made a beeline for Quint as he slowly exited his clunker.

"Sorry to keep you waiting. I had to prep for the lunch shift so Pele could take over while I'm needed here and then the requests for help didn't end until most of the customers were gone," Chef said, waving his arms in the air. By the time he reached Quint, the man's cheeks were ruddy.

"I just got here," Quint responded.

Chef offered a firm handshake. Quint could see how easily it would be to like the man. He had a calm demeanor and seemed genuine.

"I can't get the thing to fire up anymore. The screen went black and won't come back no matter what I do," Chef said, motioning toward his home.

"Let's go inside and take a look," Quint stated. "Unless you want me to take it home with me and tinker with it there."

"No. No. I can't imagine trying to pack it up. See if there's anything you can do to save it." Chef headed toward the front door. He turned his head to one side as he put his hand on the knob. "No locks needed here in Cricket Creek." True to his word, he opened the door without a key.

"Nice thing about a small town," Quint agreed. "My wife and I are from the Houston area, so we still keep everything locked. Cars. Cabin door. It's a force of habit."

"Life here is an adjustment," Chef agreed. "I moved here two years ago after owning my own restaurant in Dallas. I got jumped one morning on my way to the farmers market and decided no more. I reached out to a few friends and one connected me with Charley. It's been a quiet life for me ever since. Once I got out of the hospital."

Chef turned around and lifted his sleeve to reveal a four-inch scar.

"Knife?" Quint asked.

"From my own restaurant. One of my bar customers was arrested two days later," he said. "The guy came in every Thursday night for three months. Barely spoke to anyone and ordered the same meal every week. Seemed nice enough but I guess he was casing the place." Chef shrugged.

"That's a nasty scar," Quint agreed. He lifted one leg of his jeans to reveal a similar mark from a gash on his shin four inches above the boot. "Glass coffee table shattered on a move."

Chef winced in sympathy and the attempt to establish common ground seemed to do its trick. The man's shoulders relaxed as he nodded. "Tough business."

"Especially when a piano fights back," Quint said with a chuckle.

"Ree told me." Chef winced again.

"There's a reason it's for young men," Quint quipped. He motioned toward his boot. "But this one helped me realize how ready I am for a desk job."

"The moving world's loss is my gain," Chef said. "Let's see what I can do."

The inside of Chef's home looked a lot like the outside. There were vases of fresh flowers on most surfaces and the place could be described as tidy. The decor might be simple and clean, but it had a nice aesthetic.

"The second bedroom is my office," Chef said as he walked down a short hallway. The door was open and the room barely big enough to accommodate a desk, chair and bookshelves along one wall where a closet might have once been.

"I'm guessing this is the offending computer." Quint motioned toward the desktop.

"That she is," Chef stated.

"By the way, the chicken and waffles were the best things I've eaten all year," Quint said with a lot of enthusiasm. He wasn't kidding and it probably showed. He'd learned a long time ago to be as authentic as possible while undercover. It really was the best way to sell himself. Staying as true to himself as he possibly could was key. Otherwise he ran the risk of tripping himself up with a lie.

"Music to my ears." Chef's grin was almost ear to ear.

"Okay, so I'll start with the obvious." Quint made his way around the desk and checked the power outlet to make certain the cord hadn't jiggled loose. His initial thoughts on Chef was that the man was innocent. He had a traumatic experience in a bigger city then chose to move where he could keep his door unlocked. The probability this man was involved in bringing crime to this town was slim. Still, Quint might find something on the man's employer on the computer. "It is plugged in."

"I didn't even think to check," Chef admitted, hovering at the door.

Quint pushed the power button. "It's looking like the system is booting up and the fans are spinning." This was going to be an easier fix than he'd hoped. "Looks like a monitor issue or the graphics card died."

"How will you tell the difference?" Chef asked.

Quint checked to ensure the monitor was plugged in. "Ah, here's the problem. The video cable from the computer to the monitor has become loose."

After he corrected the problem, the screen came alive.

"I think we've solved the mystery," Quint said with a smile. He was hoping to really get inside the system before he found a solution, but this was where it ended.

Get ready to relax and indulge with your **FREE BOOKS** and more!

Claim up to FOUR NEW BOOKS & TWO MYSTERY GIFTS – absolutely FREE!

Dear Reader,

We both know life can be difficult at times. That's why it's important to treat yourself so you can relax and recharge once in a while.

And I'd like to help you do this by sending you this amazing offer of up to FOUR brand new full length FREE BOOKS that WE pay for.

This is everything I have ready to send to you right now:

Try **Harlequin® Romantic Suspense** books featuring heart-racing page-turners with unexpected plot twists and irresistible chemistry that will keep you guessing to the very end.

Try **Harlequin Intrigue® Larger-Print** books featuring action-packed stories that will keep you on the edge of your seat. Solve the crime and deliver justice at all costs.
Or **TRY BOTH!**

All we ask in return is that you answer 4 simple questions on the attached Treat Yourself survey. You'll get **Two Free Books** and **Two Mystery Gifts** from each series you try, *altogether worth over $20*! Who could pass up a deal like that?

Sincerely,

Pam Powers

Harlequin Reader Service

Treat Yourself to Free Books and Free Gifts.

Answer 4 fun questions and get rewarded.

▼ DETACH AND MAIL CARD TODAY! ▼

	YES	NO
1. I LOVE reading a good book.	◯	◯
2. I indulge and "treat" myself often.	◯	◯
3. I love getting FREE things.	◯	◯
4. Reading is one of my favorite activities.	◯	◯

TREAT YOURSELF • Pick your 2 Free Books...

Yes! Please send me my Free Books from each series I select and Free Mystery Gifts. I understand that I am under no obligation to buy anything, as explained on the back of this card.

Which do you prefer?

❏ **Harlequin® Romantic Suspense** 240/340 HDL GRCZ
❏ **Harlequin Intrigue® Larger-Print** 199/399 HDL GRCZ
❏ **Try Both** 240/340 & 199/399 HDL GRDD

FIRST NAME

LAST NAME

ADDRESS

APT.#

CITY

STATE/PROV.

ZIP/POSTAL CODE

EMAIL ❏ Please check this box if you would like to receive newsletters and promotional emails from Harlequin Enterprises ULC and its affiliates. You can unsubscribe anytime.

© 2022 HARLEQUIN ENTERPRISES ULC
™ and ® are trademarks owned by Harlequin Enterprises ULC. Printed in the U.S.A.

HI/HRS-520-TY22

"Well, that sure turned out to be easy?" Chef chuckled, walking over to stand behind Quint. "Looks like I need to stay in my lane working the kitchen."

"I'll tell you all my computer tricks if you share your batter for those chicken and waffles," Quint joked.

"Not a chance," the slightly older man shot back. "I'd rather throw my computer out and start over than give away one of my family recipes. But my creditors will thank you for me being able to pay my bills now."

Quint stood up and stepped away from the driver's seat. "It's all yours now. Pay away."

"I can't thank you enough for helping me," Chef said.

"It really was nothing," Quint argued. "But let me know if you have any other trouble with it."

"You might live to regret that offer," Chef stated with a laugh. His demeanor was casual as Quint had messed around on the computer. Another sign the man didn't have anything to hide on there.

A quick glance at the screen said the house and yard was where the tidiness ended. The desktop was cluttered with shortcuts to bank accounts, apps and games.

"I better get back home." Quint glanced at his watch. "Online class starts in an hour."

"Take this with you." Chef hurried into the kitchen, urging Quint to follow. "I baked a loaf of sourdough for you and Ree. It'll pair nicely with this minestrone soup." He pulled a decent-sized container from his fridge.

"There's no way I'll refuse food from you, Chef," Quint quipped, taking the offerings.

Then Chef handed over a bottle of wine. "The fruity notes in this chardonnay will be the perfect complement to this meal. Light a candle and voilà." Chef winked. "Insta-date."

"You're sure making my job easier with my wife," Quint said with a smile. "I appreciate this."

"It's the least I can do," Chef said. "And my name is Lorenzo Rocco. Everyone at the restaurant calls me Chef."

"Pleasure to meet you, Lorenzo." Quint glanced down at his haul. "I'd offer to shake hands but I don't have a free one at the moment."

Lorenzo got a kick out of the comment. "I'll grab the door for you."

"If you know anyone else who might need help, I'd appreciate a referral," Quint said before thanking Lorenzo again.

"You got it," Lorenzo said.

Quint unloaded his gifts into the passenger seat of his vehicle. He glanced at the yellow sports car with a little bit of envy.

The thought of a date night with Ree felt a little better than it should while working together on an investigation. Quint had never been unprofessional a day in his life and had no plans to start now, no matter how interesting and incredible Ree might be. Dating another agent crossed a line he had no intention of violating. He could use a friend, though. It wasn't until he talked to Ree that he'd realized how much of his and Tessa's lives had been entwined. He and Tessa had become inseparable. Losing her had been the equivalent of cutting off his lifeline.

Plus, there was the whole bit about Ree believing none of the passion in his kisses could be real. His second mistake slapped him in the face as he claimed the driver's seat. Was she already in a relationship? She'd asked him before. Why hadn't he done the same? According to her file, she was single. Didn't mean she wasn't in a relationship. He made a mental note to ask the next time they brought up their personal lives. He hadn't wanted to know earlier, thinking the less he knew about her personally the easier it would be to keep her at a distance.

Why did the thought of Ree being committed to someone else feel like a gut punch?

A few reasons came to mind. He'd opened up to her about Tessa. Quint also found that he actually liked talking to Ree.

Shoving the thoughts aside, he focused back on Lorenzo. In Quint's experience, a man who had something to hide locked his doors. Based on Quint's assessment of Lorenzo's openness and general disposition, he moved over to the witness list.

The other person of interest from the kitchen was Fender, the food expeditor. Then there was the mystery men from last night.

Maybe the bug in Ree's purse could turn up a clue.

Chapter Eleven

Ree finished another ache-inducing, foot-breaking shift, deciding she needed to buy some of those boot inserts from Dr. Scholl's. Quint waited at the door, as usual, as she made her exit. Her chest squeezed at seeing him standing there and warmth flooded her body.

This time, when he greeted her, he threw his arm around her neck and walked her to the cabin without a kiss. It was probably for the best. A person shouldn't get used to being kissed so thoroughly by another agent. Plus, they'd successfully sold the lie about being a couple. No one seemed suspicious in the least about their relationship status.

When he unlocked and then opened the door, she gasped.

"Where did you get all this?" she asked. The table was set; candles were lit. There were roses on the table.

"Grappell finished your social media page this afternoon. He pieced together a few pictures but thought we should have recent ones about embarking on our new life," Quint said. "He wants us to take one tonight."

"Good idea," she said, tamping down her disappointment. "I'll just change out of this uniform and throw it in the wash. Be right back." She set her phone on the table. "Why don't you go ahead and set up the shot you want."

This wasn't a real relationship. She and Quint weren't newlyweds. They weren't even friends in real life. He was a veteran agent and she was fortunate enough to get to work with him. Blurring the lines between work and real life wouldn't be good for her. Then again, Ree's mother would be happy to point out that at thirty-six years old, Ree had no life outside of work and no prospects of giving the woman grandchildren.

Ree washed the heavier makeup off her face with a makeup wipe, changed into a sundress and threw in a load of laundry.

"Once we get the picture, we can turn the lights on," Quint said as she joined him in the main living space. "Not much happened on my visit to Lorenzo's house."

She shot him a confused look. Then it seemed to dawn on her who he was actually talking about. "I'm so used to calling him Chef at work."

"Right now, let's get the shot for Grappell," Quint said through gritted teeth.

Ree took in a deep breath and turned on the camera feature on her phone with a swipe, wishing she'd brushed her hair while she was in the bathroom. With the roses, the candles and the bottle of wine that had beads of sweat from being chilled in the fridge and then set on the table, she couldn't help but wish this was reality. The setup was convincing enough.

She snapped a couple of shots of the table by itself so that she could find the best one. Then she took a selfie in front of the table. And then she brought Quint in for the shot.

He stood behind her, his masculine frame dwarfing her. She leaned into his muscled chest and her stomach free-fell. She tried to convince herself it was just the mood that had her wishing this was real. It had been a long time since she'd been on a romantic date like this one. She couldn't remember the last Valentine's Day she'd spent with someone.

Reaching back, she found Quint's hand and brought it around just under her breasts. She held on to him. It took a few seconds for her to realize how tight her grip was. Nerves?

There was no reason for them. This was nothing more than a photo shoot. Try to tell that to her senses every time she breathed in his warm, spicy scent.

"Okay. Hold still," she said, lifting the phone for the couple selfie. She snapped the pic but didn't immediately move. Neither did he. She could, however, feel his heartbeat thumping wildly against her. The frantic rhythm matched her own.

Suddenly, her throat dried up. She tried to swallow but it was basically a desert in there.

Pulling on all her strength, she cleared her throat and took a step forward.

"I got it," she said, and the air in the room suddenly became all kinds of awkward. "Um, should I send the pictures to Grappell or do you want to?"

"They're on your phone," Quint said, turning away from her. He walked over and flipped on the light like it was nothing, but a storm brewed behind those sapphire blues. It was more than a little satisfying that he seemed affected every time they got too close.

"Lorenzo seems innocent," he said, taking a seat at the table before ladling out soup.

"I get the same feeling," she said, taking a chair opposite him after tapping the screen a few times in a flurry. She sent the pictures, so that was good. Time to get her emotions under control and her head back in the game. "Is that sourdough bread?"

"Made fresh for us, apparently," Quint said and his voice came across with the same emotion as someone reading the ingredients on a cereal box. "I have a good impression of the guy." He explained his reasoning.

"This all smells amazing," she said, taking a few seconds to process the shift. "And I do, too."

Quint nodded as he dug into the soup. "Minestrone."

"I could tell," she said. "What about the bug in my purse? Did you get anything there?"

"All I can tell you is that when Charley doesn't want anyone to hear what is being said in the breakroom he turns up music and talks too low to be audible," he said.

"Not exactly the actions of an innocent man," she noted.

"No, they are not," he confirmed.

"But that also tells me you didn't get anything to work with," she stated. "Maybe I can take the trash out and drop a bug outside. There's no way Fender and Charley are only discussing waitresses and how the shift went when they go out there."

"Absolutely not," he said so quickly it almost made her head spin.

"I could—"

"Implicate yourself and give away our whole operation. Do you know how many undercover missions I've had to abort in my career?" he asked.

"No, but I didn't know there'd be a pop quiz, either," she quipped, not appreciating how cold he was suddenly being toward her.

For a split second she saw his jaw muscle tick, and that was not a good sign. Then he shook his head and seemed to laugh to himself. She sure wished he'd let her in on the joke. The temperature around this man could change in a heartbeat.

That wasn't entirely fair but she ran with it anyway. It shouldn't hurt her feelings that he'd snapped back into professional mode.

"The answer is one," Quint said. "It was my rookie year and I made a promise it would never happen again. Because do you know what happens when a cover is blown?"

"The case is abandoned," she said.

"And guilty jerks get to walk free," he added. "They

often relocate and it can take years to get anything on them again."

"What about Tessa's case?" she asked without making eye contact.

"We busted the small guys. The lower tier on a crime ring out of Romania," he said.

"Weapons? Trafficking?" she asked.

"Weapons," he said.

"I've heard about a few other Romanian rings. None of it has been good," she admitted.

"This group seemed harder than the others. If one of their own became sick while crossing the border or moving weapons, they literally shot them and dumped the body," he said.

She shivered. "That's ruthless."

"A-12 is the group we spent weeks cracking. And we got in, too. Drugs were involved so DEA showed up on bust day. It quickly became clear there were some political ties to this case, considering the multi-agency approach. The governor needed a win against them to counter the fact crime was rising in the state," he explained. "So, yeah, it got complicated."

"Sounds like you arrested A-12," she said, tucking a stray strand of hair behind her ear.

He nodded. "I've always felt like it was the tip of the iceberg, though. One of our informants gave us the name Dumitru before it all went down. Once the dust settled, I checked back. No one arrested went by that name. I've always had a niggling feeling we caught the small fry and missed the big fish. The night of the bust, a motorcycle was parked out front.

It was gone by the time the ambulance arrived. A window was open in the middle of January during a cold front, which we all know never happens at night in Texas. Someone else was there and the five guys we arrested seemed worried about going to jail."

"Isn't that normal?" she asked.

He fished his phone out of his pocket and pulled up a file. "Take a look at this."

She studied the information for a long moment.

"Each of the five died in prison within two weeks of each other," she said.

"Two were suspected to have committed suicide. Two were killed. The last guy was put in solitary confinement for his own protection. Guess what happened? He was poisoned. How did they get to him there?" He set the phone down in between them. "No one went to trial."

"So no one could roll over on anyone else," she surmised.

"Exactly. I know I was distracted once Tessa was shot. I can wholeheartedly admit that all my energy went into saving her once the place was secured. But I can't shake the look on the perps' faces when they looked at each other after we arrested them and walked them out," he said. "They seemed resigned to die."

"And that's exactly what happened," she stated. "All very interesting."

He nodded.

"I'm guessing you didn't leave the investigation alone," she said. "What else did you find?"

"Not much," he said. "The trail died with the five guys who were arrested. I shopped the name Dumitru around but have been told by every informant I've ever known that he either doesn't exist or left the country."

"But you don't believe it?" she asked.

"It's a convenient excuse," he said. "Here's the rub. The minute I bring the name up, people get real uncomfortable. Every single time."

"Which means they're scared." She was a quick study.

"Terrified. One of my trustiest guys asked me never to bring that name up around him again. Right after he told me the guy probably went back to Romania," he said.

"I'm sorry," she said. "What happened to the informant who gave you the name Dumitru in the first place?"

"I don't know. No one has seen or heard from him since," he stated.

"Why am I not surprised?" She also realized how much Quint would want to nail this jerk.

Quint stood up and then cleared the dishes from the table. Ree set her phone screen-side down before joining him.

"I got this," he said.

"I'd like to help," she countered. "I feel like I'm getting off too easy around here."

"You're doing all the heavy lifting, remember?" he asked.

"I'm making decent tips," she quipped, retrieving a bankroll from her handbag. She sat down at the table and started counting. "Too bad we don't get to keep any of this."

He smiled.

"Nope. But you can hang on to it for a while until we have to turn it over," he said.

"I'm only working the dinner shift tomorrow, by the way," she said. "The waitress I've been covering for is coming back to work. I figured you and I could run some errands. Grab lunch in town. See if we can meet any more locals."

"Good ideas," he said.

"It's what young couples do who've just relocated to a new area. They make friends," she said.

"Sounds awful," he quipped.

"I'm more of a movie person when I get a night off. Unless there's something to do," she said.

"Like what?"

"I don't know. A concert is nice. I like festivals," she said before adding, "but not ones involving eating or tossing a cricket, cooked or stuffed."

"There's a German beer festival called Wurstfest that's in New Braunfels every year," he said. "Have you been?"

"Are you kidding? Of course, I have. It's one of my grandfather's favorites," she said, practically beaming at the mention of her grandfather. It wasn't hard to realize the two were close. Then again, in a family with four boys and one girl, she was probably his princess. Losing her father must have done a number on the family and had to be the reason for her mother's concerns over Ree's chosen line of work. "Did you know it started out being called Sausage Festival?"

"Glad that name didn't last," he quipped, thinking it was a little too easy to talk to Ree.

Then again, he could use a friend even though the annoying voice in the back of his head tried to tell him the ship had sailed.

"Seriously, though," she said with a laugh that caused his heart to squeeze. When the dishes were done, he turned to find her staring at him. She immediately dropped her gaze.

"So, what about you?" He figured it was now or never. "You asked me if I was in a relationship. Are you?"

Quint suddenly felt beads of sweat form on his forehead as he waited for her answer. It wasn't like he and Ree had a relationship outside of this case. He shook it off, figuring he was just missing his friend a little too much lately. The six-month anniversary of Tessa's death was around the corner.

"No," she said before standing and mumbling something about taking a shower.

Why did his heart hammer against his ribs at the thought of her being available?

Chapter Twelve

Ree finished her shower in record time, trying her best not to think about Quint's question. Why did admitting to him there was no one special in her life stir all kinds of mixed emotions? Rather than focus on something she had no control over, she wished there was something she could do to help Quint get answers on Dumitru. Maybe then he could get closure?

She toweled off, brushed her teeth and then moved her clothes from the washer to the stackable dryer in the hall closet. Thankfully, the cabin had laundry or she would be in a world of hurt trying to handwash her uniform every night.

Her shift had been a real winner. Two tables had stiffed her on a tip despite her giving them amazing service. Adrian had shrugged and said it happened from time to time, but at least Ree was getting Adrian to open up more. She'd said Ree must've drawn the short stick on customers. Even so, Ree earned a wad of cash that she kept balled up with a rubber band. Best not to leave it in her purse, so she tucked it inside a coffee mug and replaced it in the back of the cabinet.

"What should we do tomorrow?" she asked. Quint's gaze was focused on the screen as the sounds of squeaky truck brakes cut across the parking lot. The temptation to run to the window was real. She took in a deep breath and resisted.

Quint's gaze flew to the window.

"Don't worry. The camera will capture the activity," he reassured her, as though he could read her mind. Then again, he was the one with all the experience. Her instincts were good, she realized that right away. But she lacked practice.

"Right," she said, trying not to think about all the mistakes she'd made today alone. Adrian wasn't as chatty after Ree had started asking questions. She'd made a judgment about Chef's innocence and now it was difficult to keep her objectivity with him. At least Quint had the same impression. But she doubted he would let that get in the way of keeping an objective eye on the man. All she wanted to do was keep asking. "I wonder if I should push Adrian for a little more information."

"What do your instincts tell you?" he asked casually.

"To back off. But I want to charge ahead," she said. "There's so much we don't know, and I feel like a sit-down lunch or a reason to have drinks with Adrian could clear up a whole lot."

"Or draw attention to us," he stated.

"There is that," she acquiesced. "I'm also wondering if I should nudge Charley about considering me to be a barmaid since progress is slow with the other waitresses."

"Being too eager might cause Charley to back away from you instead of bring you in closer," he said. He was right and she knew it before he said the words. Still, she wanted to do something more than wait on tables and Charley's 'friends' seemed to like the bar.

"What else did Chef say today?" she asked, tapping her finger on the table.

"I wasn't there for long enough for him to say too much. If it was a test, which I highly doubt, then I seem to have passed," he said. "I couldn't dig into his files since it was a cord issue and not a bigger problem. If I'm honest, I'd hoped to be able to take a look around. But I established trust and that's important."

"Yes, it is," she agreed.

"Looks like I'm up," Quint said, pushing up to standing. "It won't take me long to shower."

Why did those words send warmth swirling low in her belly?

Mentally shaking off her reaction, she cleared her throat. She thought about her last relationship, and was reminded how bad she was at them. There'd been good qualities to her ex. For instance, they'd known each other for a long time, so they were comfortable together. Being away from him reminded her of all the good times they'd shared.

Had Shane been right? Did she keep her running

shoes at the door? Was it time to start dating with a different attitude?

Preston was the only person from her past she could see herself going there with. Maybe she should give him a call after this assignment. Or not. The few fights they'd had were over her commitment to work. He'd framed one of them as her lack of commitment to their relationship but he'd been saying the same thing in different ways…he wanted to be her priority over work.

Ree had been up front with him. She'd explained that she was building her career and that it had to take precedence for now. She'd explained that it wouldn't always be this way, and that once she got established there'd be time for more. Preston had been clear on his stance. He wasn't willing to wait it out.

Curiosity had her wondering what had changed. He had to realize her priorities were still the same. If anything, she was deeper into her work now than before she got her last promotion. Going undercover was an even bigger commitment. Was that the reason she was reaching back for the familiar? She was so outside her comfort zone right now? And had been for the last year?

She didn't know how to grow without pushing herself. Work had to be a priority. There would be plenty of time for a spouse and possibly kids later on down the road. An odd realization struck. Did she even want kids? The honest truth was that she didn't know. She hadn't given much thought to her personal life. It just seemed like she had time.

Had Tessa thought the same thing?

The question struck like stray lightning on a sunny summer day. Didn't everyone take for granted that tomorrow was a given? Despite being in a dangerous line of work, Ree never once questioned that she would come home at the end of the day or assignment. Her mother, on the other hand, reminded Ree far too often how risky the job was.

At least her grandfather had nothing but confidence in her.

Was Ree being naive to think nothing could ever happen to her on the job?

Probably a little, at the very least. Then again, worrying never solved a problem, either. And if she didn't believe with every fiber of her being that she would come home every night she'd probably picked the wrong line of work.

If Preston was reaching out to Shane, did that mean he'd come to accept her priorities? She could see herself doing long-term with him if he could give her space to develop her career and to figure out if she wanted to have a family or not.

Rather than stew on that any longer when she didn't have any clear answers, she shifted gears. There was something niggling at the back of her mind about this whole investigation, and she had yet to pinpoint exactly what it was. A distraction would be nice. Or maybe she just needed sleep because her thoughts kept circling back to the kisses she'd shared with Quint and the disappointment burning in her chest at the lack of them tonight.

Getting sleep just jumped up a few notches on her priority scale. She settled under the covers, trying her level best not to think about Quint. And mostly succeeded.

As she closed her eyes, he came out of the bathroom. The lights were dim. She pretended to be asleep, figuring this wasn't the time to speak to the man she couldn't seem to shake from her thoughts when she should be thinking about a man she might actually have a shot at a future with.

Rather than beat that dead horse, she rolled onto her side and tried to go to sleep.

Ten minutes ticked by and all she'd done so far was roll from side to side. She heard the occasional click-click-clack of fingers on a keyboard, and wondered what Quint was up to. This was the point in the day when he examined footage.

When she couldn't stand faking being asleep for another second, she sat up. "Find anything yet?"

"Is everything okay?" he asked, not sounding as caught off guard as she'd suspected he might. "Why aren't you asleep?"

"Can't." She didn't think this was the time to go into the fact she was torn between thinking about her on-again, off-again boyfriend and Quint. She sat up and hugged her knees into her chest. "Are you getting anything?"

"I'm not seeing anything big enough to carry weapons, no matter how hard I'm trying. There's no activity to suggest crates of guns are moving through here," he admitted. "There's something here, though. There has to be. We just haven't found it yet."

"I'm not seeing anything illegal or immoral going on inside, either," she said on a sigh.

"What are we missing?" He tapped his fingers on the sofa's armrest. His cell buzzed and it seemed to catch them both by surprise. He retrieved his phone and checked the screen. "Looks like today was more productive than we thought. Charley is asking if I can come in tomorrow and take a look at his computer. Said Lorenzo couldn't stop talking about what I did for him."

Was this the break they needed?

Chapter Thirteen

Quint figured his strategy of staying away from the restaurant had worked. He was beginning to question whether this establishment was the center for crime the informant had made it out to be, though. The information had come from a credible source, so he was surprised nothing had turned up so far. Then again, his luck might just be about to change.

Coffee in hand, he headed over to the restaurant at 9:00 a.m. as Charley had requested in their text exchange last night before bed. Leaving the cabin while Ree slept had him slipping out the door quietly. The second thing on his mind this morning was her single relationship status. It wasn't any of Quint's business, but he'd asked the question anyway. Then again, maybe that was where she drew the line between work and relationships.

Work was work. Home was home. Quint had a similar philosophy. His went more like he didn't work where he lived. In a job such as theirs, it was easy to blur the lines. Good for her if she'd made the division this early in her career. Becoming best friends with his partner had taken away his objectivity about her. If the two of them hadn't been so personal with each other, Tessa would be holding her baby in her arms right now instead of being buried with her.

The dark thought soured Quint's mood as he opened the front door of Greenlight. He walked inside, shouting a hello. The doors to the kitchen were propped open. Charley appeared, waving Quint back.

"Thank you for coming. Lorenzo is still embarrassed all you had to do was plug in a cord. He did nothing but sing your praises." Charley offered a firm handshake. Quint took note of the man's cold and clammy hand. Was he nervous?

"I don't know about that," Quint stated. "I'm still a work in progress on that front but I'd much rather learn how a computer works than move another one."

Charley laughed at the joke. Good. The trick to working with a creep was to focus on their good qualities and they always had some. Quint had once had to get close to a man who'd murdered his own mother. But the guy loved his fourteen-year-old kid, who was in juvie at the time. So much so, in fact, that the murderer was willing to roll over on a drug operation in exchange for a lenient sentence for his boy. No one was either all good or all bad. Quint had learned to concentrate on the good.

"My books are a mess and my inventory is based on what's in here." He pointed to his head. "I've been told there is a way to automate all this so I'm not doing manual counts. Have you heard of any of this?"

"There are accounting software programs for small businesses that should help with the books," Quint stated. "I hear some even link up to inventory and can place orders for you when stock is down based on what dishes are being sold. But I'm not sure if that is too complicated for what you're looking for."

"I like the idea of help with the books. What about starting there?" Charley asked.

"Fine," Quint said. He was surprised Charley would give access to his books to anyone outside the company, but Lorenzo's endorsement seemed to go a long way.

"How should we go about this?" Charley asked, then said, "First things first, I'd like for you to take a look at how I'm set up now and see what you can improve on."

"Sounds like as good a place as any to start," he said. "I have a ten-thirty class, which gives me an hour or so to get the lay of the land."

Being too available could raise a red flag, Quint knew from experience. Seeming too eager could raise another one. Patience won every time.

Charley's eyes widened for a second in surprise, but then he nodded. "You could come back at any time. Set your own schedule."

"Sounds good. I'll have to do a bit of research to figure out which program would be best. I can also ask one of my professors." Quint added the last part for effect.

Charley kept nodding. He seemed to like what he was hearing.

"I'd like to pay you something for your efforts," Charley said. "Not sure what the going rate is."

"You're keeping my wife employed," Quint countered.

"Still. If you do work for me then you should get paid," Charley said.

"Since I'm still in training, how about you pay me with dinners on the house?" he asked, motioning toward his stool from the other night. "Then, I get to see my bride while I eat."

"Dinner's the least I can do," Charley said. "But we'll start there."

"I've already had a few meals from here. Believe me when I say I'm on the good side of this deal." Quint winked.

The smile on Charley's face said he was proud of his restaurant's reputation for good food. Interesting, though, because while he seemed to care about Greenlight, he was also risking his business by running guns out the back. Or was this being done right underneath his nose? Fender, the expeditor, came to mind. Or it could be a supplier. Or both. Phillip was another mystery.

However, Charley was no saint. The question was whether or not he was involved in other crimes that were feeding into a bigger crime ring.

"Follow me." Charley walked to a small office in front of the breakroom on the left-hand side of the kitchen. It wasn't much bigger than a good-sized closet. A custom-fitted desk with stacks of paper-work on top gave the place a distinctly cluttered feel. There was literally something on every surface, which didn't give him a whole lot of confidence the man's computer desktop was any better.

Quint's house was a complete contrast to this. Some folks might call his decor minimalist, but he didn't collect more than he could use at the time. When he was done with something, he donated it, pitched it, or gave it away.

He cracked his knuckles and looked toward Quint. "No time like the present to get started."

Charley grabbed a piece of paper and tore off a corner. He shuffled a few stacks of papers before locating a pen. "Here are the passwords you'll need." He scribbled a few down and Quint could only hope he could read the handwriting. "Ignore all the curse words. This is what happens when a place keeps kicking back my attempts."

That made Quint laugh.

"I'll be back but you have my phone number if you need anything," Charley said.

"Sounds good. I'll play around in here. See what can be optimized and what can be eliminated," he said. This very well could be a test to see if he could be trusted alone at the restaurant. So Quint would play it cool. In all this clutter, there could be a tiny camera or listening device planted somewhere. Today meant taking a huge step in this case. Cool was the only way to play it. "We can start with the basics."

"Like making sure you have all the right utensils before you start cooking?" Charley surmised.

"Basically, but more like making sure we have a building with a fridge, ovens, etc. before we open our restaurant," Quint explained.

Charley seemed to take to the line of thinking. His grin was wide, and he kept nodding. "I never looked at the computer like that before. It helps me understand its usefulness when you put it like that."

"Score one for technology," Quint said, trying to capitalize on the light mood.

"I'll leave you to it," Charley said. The vibes with this guy were mixed. The intel versus what they were witnessing didn't add up. The expectation he ran a hardcore criminal operation out the back door didn't seem to be panning out.

Quint nodded before taking a seat and grabbing the scrap of paper. The passwords were the best part. There was quite an education in creative cussing built into those.

Maybe he could finally dig around enough to either find something on this guy or think about moving on from this investigation and calling it a bust. The system booted up fine. Much like the small office Quint was in, the computer's desktop was a cluttered mess. Icons littered the screen. At least the guy had a PC instead of a Mac, so the icons were on a grid. That made it a little bit easier to make sense of them.

First things first: no one needed this much disarray on a desktop. Before Quint could rearrange the icons and clean it up, he needed to figure out which ones were actually being used and also useful for Charley.

Quint made a show of studying the screen. He nodded his head a few times in case there were cameras. Based on what he saw with the desktop, no one around here knew what they were doing with technology.

The first thing he did, though, was uninstall the virus protection software. Next, he built a custom firewall. By the time he finished, his "class" would be starting in fifteen minutes. He located a sticky note pad and a pen, and then jotted down the two changes he'd made before sticking the yellow square on the bottom of the screen. He also opened a new spreadsheet, saved the file to the desktop and recorded the date along with his actions for future reference. He glanced at the payroll versus the schedule and noted the barmaids were paid under the table.

It was too early to install spy software. He needed to get a better lay of the land first. That was okay. This was progress.

And now he needed to get home to update his "wife" on his progress. His heart skipped a couple of beats thinking about her and how beautiful she was with her long silky waves spilled across the pillow.

Quint gave himself a mental headshake to clear the sexy, sleepy image of Ree as he walked out into the sun and toward the cabin.

REE FIXED A BAGEL. There was cream cheese and jelly, her favorites. She slathered them both on as soon as her bagel popped out of the toaster, and then poured a cup of freshly brewed coffee. She didn't mind doing these things for herself, so it must just be Quint's presence that she missed.

Shaking off the thought, she moved to the table and checked her phone. No messages from Quint.

The door opened, and she was a little happier than she should be that Quint was back. He immediately closed and locked the door before toeing off one boot. He unstrapped himself from the other at the door, leaving them both beside the door.

"Good morning," she said as he turned around to face her.

He took two steps forward before his gaze dropped to her plate. His face momentarily lost all color. "I thought you liked eggs."

"Thought I'd change it up today," she said, unsure why he would care about her breakfast.

"Okay," was all he said before heading over to the coffee machine. He poured a cup as she sat there, dumbfounded.

"Could you explain to me what just happened?" she asked, not ready to let him off the hook.

He shook his head as he turned around and then leaned his hip against the counter. "I had a good meeting with Charley this morning."

Apparently, they were changing the subject.

"What about his computer? Did you get anything to work with there?" she asked.

"Not yet. I'm getting the lay of the land first," he

said. "But I do have a sense of how the man works. Disorganized."

"Not when it comes to his restaurant," she said. "The walk-in freezer has to be organized a particular way. Same goes for the fridges."

"Isn't that Lorenzo's domain?" he asked.

"Yes, but I get the impression Charley would have a fit if everything wasn't just so," she said. "He checks everything despite having what appears to be full trust in Chef." She flashed eyes at him. "Lorenzo."

"Charley's office and desktop are the complete opposite," he stated. "So that's interesting. It signals a person who cares about the details of his business. In my experience those folks aren't usually criminals, so it will be interesting to see how this all plays out. Also, the barmaids are not on payroll."

"Oh. Really? Other than dating new-hire waitresses, I agree with everything you've said about Charley, Quint." She picked up the bagel, took a bite and then chewed.

Quint took a sip of his coffee.

"I haven't seen any trucks out back that look like they could be carrying in weapons. We're at square one, but it's still early. I'm gaining trust. I might be able to install spyware tomorrow morning," he said.

"Is that the schedule?" she asked. "Are you going back every morning?"

"That's what we agreed on so far," he said. She couldn't pinpoint the difference but there was a subtle change in Quint. Was this always the case when he went deeper undercover? She wanted to ask but figured this wasn't the time. Not when she was picking up on a strange vibe from him.

"Do you want a bagel?" she offered, trying to find some middle ground.

"No. And I'd prefer if you didn't make yours that way but I can't force you to do anything you don't want to," he said through gritted teeth.

"Do you mind telling me what about my breakfast has offended you to this degree?" Or was it just her in general he seemed offended by?

"You can eat whatever you want. I'd just prefer not to watch." He walked over to the sofa, set down his coffee and grabbed his laptop.

"If you didn't want me to eat this…why did you buy all the ingredients?" she asked, frustration making her unable to let it go.

She should be able to get past it but she couldn't. He studied the screen without looking up at her.

"Are you serious right now?" she asked. "You're not talking to me?"

When Quint brought his gaze up to her it was like all hell came up with him. "If you must know, that was Tessa's favorite breakfast. I bought those ingredients separately, not thinking anyone else ate like her. My bad."

"I had no idea," she said, refusing to feel bad for something she didn't know would be a trigger. This was what it would be like to live with a ghost.

Chapter Fourteen

"It's my fault," Quint said, realizing his mistake. "I shouldn't have snapped at you. To be fair, I didn't want to talk about it at all. I owe you an apology."

"Nope. You sure shouldn't. But I accept," she agreed. Her lips formed a thin line. "I need to get some air." She picked up her plate, and then walked right out the door.

Quint sat there, unsure of his next move. They weren't a couple, and he didn't owe her any explanations on his personal life. So why did he feel like the biggest jerk on earth? Again, he couldn't afford the distraction from the case.

He refocused on his plan. Tomorrow, he could dig around in a couple of apps under the guise of trying to figure out what was needed for the restaurant and what wasn't. If he clicked onto an account he wasn't supposed to, it could be easily explained as housekeeping. In a day or two, he might be able to slip spyware on the system. It was risky and he needed to make absolutely certain he wouldn't be found out.

He wrestled with another thought. Could he bug

the office without giving himself away? The clutter would make it easy to hide a listening device around the size of a fly. If it was found, though...

Quint opened his email and wrote a brief account of their progress to date before sending it over to Lynn Bjorn, the boss. Bjorn was probably in meeting after meeting and wouldn't read the email until around midnight. Quint had learned a long time ago to send anything urgent via text. His boss read emails before she logged off her home computer for the night. This didn't qualify as urgent.

Before he could stand up to check on Ree, he heard male voices outside. Quint raced to secure his "bad" foot in the boot and then slid the other one inside his walking boot. He stopped at the door and listened. There were times to interrupt a fellow agent and times it backfired or caused them to lose momentum in a good conversation.

"I'm not working the lunch shift today, fellas," she said with a voice that bordered on flirty. She might be playing a part but he didn't have to like it. He also had no right to dislike it. Officially.

He couldn't make out a response.

She said, "I doubt my husband would like that."

His chest flared with jealousy. He tried to write it off as being in character.

Ree could hold her own. Clearly. But that didn't stop him from wanting to rip open the door and tell those guys off.

"People have to eat," she said, sounding like she'd

rather poke her eyes with needles than be in this conversation. "I'll catch you guys later."

A few seconds later, the door opened, hitting him in the face.

"Oh, sorry," she said when she realized what she'd done.

"No need to apologize. I was just listening to see if you needed your 'husband' to come out and back you up." He made air quotes around the word *husband*. "The door is on me."

"Literally," she said without that trademark sense of humor of hers. However, the spark in her green eyes made him wish he could claim those pink lips again. Part of him had gone into self-preservation mode when it came to Ree. He did what he had to in order to survive.

He couldn't help but smile at her reaction, though. So he didn't try to contain his amusement. "Good one, Ree."

"That's what happens when you grow up with so many brothers. You develop a sharp tongue," she said, sticking hers out at him.

Again, he laughed at the silliness of it. She had a way of breaking through his frustration and making him smile when he probably needed to go to the gym for a couple of hours to work off his tension.

Ree possessed magic like he'd never seen before. All she had to do was make one well-timed wisecrack to break him down. Clearly, his tough-guy skills needed some work.

"All right." He rubbed the spot on his nose that took the worst hit. "Let's talk about work."

"Can't. I have to get ready for my job," she said.

"I thought the plan was to go into town and get to know the locals," he stated.

"It was, until Zoey sent me a text out of the blue asking me to switch shifts with her today." She held up her phone.

"But you just told those guys you weren't working." He must've shot a look because she wiggled her eyebrows at him.

"Did you think I wanted those Neanderthals on my shift?" she asked with a devious grin.

"You really are a force to reckon with," he said.

"Darn right," she quipped. Her smile had a way of shooting straight through a person. No wonder she had a stash of tips bigger than any bootleggers. "And I have to get ready because I don't have a whole lot of time."

"Don't let me stand in your way." He stepped aside and held his arm out like he was presenting a Ferrari at a car show.

"You couldn't. I'd never allow it," she said with more of that spark in her emerald jewels.

"No one would argue that," he said as she passed by him. "Oh, and I updated our boss. Bjorn is up to date on the progress we've made so far."

"Great." Ree disappeared into the bathroom, returning ten minutes later looking ready for her shift. He preferred her in a little more clothing if she was going to leave the cabin, but the uniform couldn't be helped. The white boots uniform showed even more skin, if that was even possible without being a swimsuit.

"You look good," he said.

"Thanks." Her eyes perked up at the compliment.

"We're a newly married couple who has been home far too much since we arrived," he said. "Since we can't have lunch in town, why don't we have dinner out instead?"

"As long as it's not Greenlight, I'll take it," she said. "Don't get me wrong, the food is amazing, but I don't want to spend my night off—"

"Don't worry. I have something much better in mind." If memory served, there was a honky-tonk, boot-scootin' bar that was more tourist attraction than authentic country dive within easy driving distance. As much as he'd rather keep her off her feet, and by that he meant like at the movies, they needed to get out and mingle, just like she'd suggested. Newlyweds rarely stayed in on the weekends.

"Is that right?" She walked over to him and grabbed a fistful of his shirt. She locked gazes and for a split second he saw her confidence falter. She recovered by clearing her throat. "How about walking a lady to work?"

"The pleasure would be mine," he said, not wanting to admit how much he liked their routine.

REE'S SHIFT FLEW by and before she knew it she was refilling ketchup bottles. There should be no surprise there, considering it was Friday. She could only imagine what kind of business the weekends would bring. The money was good. The barmaids had to be bringing in serious cash. Could they be part of the weapons ring? Quint had already confirmed none of them were on payroll.

A man walked in, wearing jeans, boots and a tan shirt with the word *Sheriff* written down one arm. Gaze intent on the kitchen door, he didn't say a word to Ree. His intensity said he was on a mission. Law enforcement officers made her nervous while she was undercover. Officers could generally spot each other half a mile away. Clothes didn't matter. The person need not be in uniform for her to clue in. There was a swagger to their walk and they always held their left arm a little too far from the body, a sign they were used to wearing a holster and accommodating space for a gun. She had to consciously do the opposite in order to untrain some of those habits.

Adrian shot a look and compressed her lips before shrugging and going back to her duties as she closed out her station. Raised voices could be heard from the back as the kitchen staff came through the dining room and then out the front door. Fender lit a smoke. He walked toward the road and away from the others as he pulled out his cell and made a call.

For a split second, Ree debated following them. Her station was closed out and there was no real reason to stick around. She waved bye to Adrian before heading out and to the cabin.

Chef Lorenzo leaned against the building, thumbing through his cell. He barely glanced up as she passed by.

"See you tomorrow," she said.

He gave her a friendly salute.

At the cabin, Quint was in the middle of a work-out session when she walked inside. His shirt was off, and he wore shorts that sat low on his hips. She couldn't tear her gaze away from a bead of sweat that rolled down his chest as he pulled up into another crunch. Muscles rippled with his movement. The man's body was made for sinning. She tried not to calculate out how long it had been since the last time she'd had sex. *Too long*, her body screamed. As tempting as it sounded to have a fling, she'd never been the one-night-stand type. For it to work for her, she had to have an emotional attachment. Different things worked for different people. She had no judgment on how other people conducted their lives. If it wasn't illegal, immoral or didn't hurt puppies, she had a live-and-let-live philosophy.

Despite her convictions, she'd never wanted to have sex with a man more than she wanted to have it with Quint in that moment.

He stood up, picked up the towel he'd been on and mumbled an apology.

"No, don't stop on my account," she said, stumbling over her words like an awkward teenager. "I need to get out of these clothes anyway. You're not going to bother me." The words flew out of her mouth at a surprising pace.

"If you're sure you don't mind," he said with a grin that said he noticed.

"Nope. It's good to keep in shape. Bodies need exercise." Well, hadn't she just handed over all the wisdom? What was she going to say next? The sky is blue? Grass is green?

Before she dug a deeper hole, she fast-walked across the room and to the bathroom where she changed out of her work clothes. She dabbed a little more pink gloss on her lips and blew out her hair. She had no idea what the plans were for tonight or what she needed to wear for them. Rather than interrupt Quint's workout for the second time, she stayed in the bathroom fixing herself up for their date.

When she could stall no longer in front of the mirror, she changed into a cream-colored minidress that she planned to wear her boots with.

Opening the door to the bathroom gave her quite a shock as Quint stood there, leaning against the wall, toweling off sweat before it dripped off his golden, sun-kissed skin. It had been a long time since anyone rattled her nerves the way he did.

She chalked it up to the stress of the mission and moved past him. "All yours."

He thanked her before she heard the door close behind her. No way did she intend to look back. Instead, she marched directly to the fridge for a Coke. The fizzle tickled her throat. Ree retrieved her cell phone and then sat at the dining room table, wishing she could have been a fly on the wall next door before her shift ended.

In the heat of the moment earlier, she'd forgotten to tell Quint about what happened at the restaurant. Could be nothing, she reassured herself. She checked the window. The sheriff's vehicle was gone. Another mistake on her part. She should have stayed focused when she walked through the door instead of getting flustered like a teenager in the same room with a pop star.

Ree checked her cell phone. Shane texted asking if all was well. She suspected her brother was checking up on her since she hadn't responded to Preston. This was exactly the reason she'd separated out her dating life from her family. Her brothers, especially Shane, hovered enough. The last thing she needed was for them to be in her business 24/7 or receiving information about her from another source. When she was ready to talk, she would.

She sighed. As great as Preston was—and he had a whole lot of wonderful qualities—she wasn't sure if she was ready to dive back into that pool. And right now wasn't the time to worry about the man.

Fresh from the shower, Quint emerged from the bathroom. She tried not to stare, or drool, as he pulled a shirt over his head and then shrugged into it.

"I forgot to tell you something when I first got home. The sheriff showed up today at the end of my shift and he didn't look thrilled. He went straight back to the office without making eye contact with anyone. The kitchen staff emptied out and Fender walked away from the others presumably to light a cigarette but he immediately made a phone call," she informed.

"Okay, the activity should be on the recording," he said, moving to the laptop on the coffee table. He took a seat on the couch and raked his fingers through still-wet hair, taming his slight curls. Was he kidding? How on earth could someone be so gorgeous with so little effort?

"I just wish I'd been a fly on the wall when the sheriff confronted his cousin," she said, still beating herself up over not remembering something so important.

"You and me both."

She issued a sharp sigh. It must have been loud because he looked up at her.

"What's wrong?" he asked.

She shook her head, not ready to admit how embarrassed she was about his half-naked body distracting her from her job.

"Whatever it is, let it go," he said.

"Do you?" she shot back.

"No. I can't say that I do. If it made me a better agent, I wouldn't be advising you to do the opposite. Since we seem to be cut from the same cloth, I'll tell you to figure out what works for you and stick to it religiously," he stated. "And if that doesn't work, hit the mat and don't stop working your body until it becomes more tired than your brain."

"Sounds like good advice," she said, wondering if that was exactly what he was doing when she walked in. She also saw how ripped the man was and realized the level of his pain must be as intense.

"Works some days better than others," he quipped,

returning his gaze to the screen. Then came, "The sheriff walked inside looking concerned and he left with a scowl on his face. He was inside the restaurant for seven minutes."

"How about Fender?" she asked.

"He stayed outside on his cell phone for another five minutes," he stated. "But it's his body language that interests me. He's waving his free arm in the air. He inhales the cigarette like there's no tomorrow."

"I never have gotten a good vibe from him," she said. "Any chance he's facing the camera?"

"I'll send this part of the video to Grappell for evaluation. See what he can do with it. He can run it through facial recognition. Fender is pacing and when he comes back this way, they might be able to blow this up and read his lips. It's too grainy for us to make anything out," he said. His fingers danced across the keyboard. "There. Now the clip is off." He shifted gears, setting the laptop aside before standing up. "Are you ready to go meet some locals?"

She nodded, hoping they could catch a break while they were out.

Chapter Fifteen

"I feel like I'm missing something here," Quint said as he parked the sedan in a sea of pickup trucks. The legendary country bar on the outskirts of town was large enough to park a fleet of semis in.

"You think?" Ree laughed, and the sound was musical. She'd calmed down considerably on the ride over. "Maybe we should have requested a pickup instead of this ride."

"We would definitely fit in better," he said with a smile.

"Am I about to learn something new about you?" she asked. "As in, you dance?"

"Believe me, I try not to," he said. "And when you see my two-step, you might take those words back."

"I'm sure you're fine at it," she said as he exited the vehicle and then came around to her side to open the door for her.

"At least I have an excuse." He pointed down to his "injured" ankle with the bright white boot strapped on it.

"So do I." She held up her left hand. "I'm pretty

sure this gold band is a romance killer for strange men."

"Who knows. It might entice them even more," he said. He'd seen, heard and encountered all kinds of things during his years as a bachelor.

"That's scary," she admitted, taking the hand he held out to her and using it as leverage to exit the sedan.

"You look beautiful tonight," he said, figuring he needed to slip into the newlywed role before they headed inside. He wasn't kidding, though. She'd taken his breath away when he walked out of the bathroom earlier.

"You're not so bad yourself," she said with a smile and those same sparkly eyes that had him wanting to do things that could get them both in trouble.

Too bad, he thought. Then again, maybe not. Mixing his personal life with work wasn't high on his priority list at the moment. Losing Tessa had hit him on too many fronts. Coworkers needed to be kept at a professional distance.

He put his right arm out for Ree to grab hold of. From the parking lot, he could already hear the music thumping inside. "Shall we?"

"Yes. And I hope they have good food because I could eat my own arm off right now." She took the offering as he broke into a laugh.

"I'm not sure how many newlyweds have the kinds of conversations we do, but it sure would make the idea of getting married a whole lot more tempting," he said, not that he planned to change his single ways any time soon. But no one could argue his point. Being with someone who made him laugh had just made his list of required traits for a serious relationship.

"Laughing is a good thing," she agreed as they walked inside.

It was the dinner hour and the place was already hopping. There was no one on the dance floor just yet but the tables surrounding the sawdust-covered wood flooring were packed. There was no cover charge. A sign near the front door read Seat Yourself.

Quint found a counter-height table on the other side of the dance floor. A couple of plastic menus were sandwiched in between condiments and a container filled with napkins.

Ree wasted no time grabbing two before handing one over to him. "I could probably eat this menu."

He couldn't help but smile. "What looks good?"

"How about we start with the ground beef nachos and then I'll have shrimp tacos," she said after a quick perusal. "And a cold beer."

The waitress turned up by the time Ree finished her sentence. She gave a quick recap.

"All of that sounds good to me. I'll have what she's having and whatever you have on tap," Quint said.

The perky twenty-ish-year-old rattled off a list of options, and he stopped her when she got to his favorite, Guinness.

"Oh, that sounds good to me, too," Ree stated with enough enthusiasm to convince him. "And water, please."

The waitress set down four cardboard squares and he figured she was marking the table to let the rest of the staff know orders had been taken. There seemed to be several waitresses buzzing around, and the casual setting had him thinking there weren't set stations.

"I'll be back with your drinks," she said before disappearing.

Quint reached across the table and took Ree's hand in his, linking their fingers. The move was meant to make a statement to others. The electricity pulsing up his hand gave the whole scenario credibility. He poured on the newlywed loving gaze as much as he could without going overboard. In another circumstance, another situation, another time, he could see himself opening up to someone like her. Ree was special. If he hadn't already done the best-friend-as-partner route and been burned about as hard as someone could be, he could also see himself going there with her.

His heart argued there were quite a few differences between the two. Tessa had been more likely to punch him in the arm or make fun of his anemic dating life. He would be more likely to be her wingman than her date. And he would defend his dating choices and frequency to the grave. So what if Tessa had told him over and over again that he should date women with more…how had she put it?…substance.

He did. There was plenty of interesting conversation. Okay, maybe not so much in the past couple of years, but he'd grown tired of the same get-to-know-each-other conversations. He could admit he'd been going through the motions lately without really putting himself out there.

The truth was that he had Tessa. The person he enjoyed hanging out with the most just happened to be the opposite sex. There were no romantic fantasies with her. Their relationship had been clearly defined from the start and had grown into a deep-seated closeness that rivaled most good marriages. Other agents had joked the two of them were like an old married couple, saying they'd skipped all the fun parts of a relationship and had ended up at the no-sex, best-friend stage of life.

Looking back, he could see they probably weren't too far off base.

"What are you thinking about?" Ree's voice sliced into his heavy thoughts.

He shrugged. "Not much, I guess."

She shot him a look that could have cut through steel. "Don't feed me that line, Quint. I'm not stupid and I have eyes. You were zoned out in thought and I wondered what was running through your mind."

Quint took in a deep breath. "Tessa. I was thinking about her."

His comment really seemed to bring down the mood.

Ree nodded and gave a small, sad smile. "You must have loved her very much."

"It would be the same if something happened to one of your brothers," he admitted. "The pain is unimaginable."

"It's unthinkable to lose someone so young and vibrant," she said. "As much as my brothers can be a pain in the backside, I can't fathom life without any one of them."

"I'm sorry about the mood shift, it's just…"

Ree shook her head. "It's okay. I actually think it's good for you to talk about her. I mean, bottling it all up inside can't be healthy."

"Yeah? I appreciate your concern but we're here for our date night. I don't want to talk about my sister any longer," he said, figuring he needed to provide a cover story in case anyone was listening. There were a dozen tables scattered around. The music was quiet enough to talk over but loud enough to make it difficult to hear anyone who wasn't standing nearby. Try as he might, he couldn't make out what anyone around him was saying unless he tried to read lips.

"Promise me you'll talk to someone about her if not to me." Her serious tone and concerned look made him think twice about what she said. He didn't want to blow her off or pretend he wasn't hurting anymore.

"Okay," he said. "I will. And I'd like the person to be you."

REE SQUEEZED QUINT's hand in a show of support, trying not to give away the effect his words had on her. One look in his eyes said he would follow through with his promise. She wouldn't mind if he talked to her about Tessa. If he wasn't comfortable enough to do that, all she really cared about was making certain he spoke to someone. No matter what else, Quint had weaved his way inside her heart in the past couple of days of being together 24/7. She cared about what happened to him beyond this assignment.

The waitress showed with drinks. The appetizer soon followed. The music started picking up tempo and volume as the shrimp tacos were served. By the time their bellies were full, a band started setting up on the stage.

"How'd you hear about this place?" she asked Quint after placing her napkin on the table to indicate she was done.

"Are you kidding me?" he shot back and she could tell he was in a much more playful mood by the tone of his voice. "How do you *not* know about Honk-E Tonk? It's one of the most famous bars in Texas after that cowboy movie ten years ago."

"I thought it was called Gillespies," she admitted.

"That was the name in the movie," he confirmed.

She glanced around from side to side, scanning the room for the infamous mechanical bull riding pen. "Where is it?"

"Upstairs." He motioned toward the wooden staircase in the corner that, now that she really looked at it, led to a loft.

"Can we do it later?" she asked before glancing down, remembering he was in a boot.

"You can," he offered. "I'll cheer you on from the sideline."

"Deal." Her heart literally gave a little flip.

"Did you get enough to eat?" he asked, gazing at

her with those loving eyes again. This man was a little too good at this undercover thing. Staring into those sapphire blues, she could get lost and trick herself into thinking this was real and not make-believe. Wouldn't do a whole lot of good to fall down that sinkhole.

Her cell buzzed just loud enough to hear over the music. She retrieved it from her purse and then checked the screen. Shane?

"It's my brother," she said to Quint. "I better take this."

He nodded as she stood up, took the call and plugged one of her ears.

"Hello?" she said into the receiver, hoping Shane could hear her over the loud music. Fear gripped her that something might be wrong back home. Shane knew she was on an assignment and wouldn't call unless there was an emergency.

"Hey, sis," Shane began calmly as she got her hand stamped before walking into the parking lot. The sun was descending, creating a bright orange glow in the sky. She thought about Quint and almost texted him to come outside, wondering if this was the exact shade of orange that was his favorite. She imagined it came pretty darn close if it wasn't a perfect match, and she saw the sheer beauty in it.

"Is everything all right?" she asked, bracing herself for bad news. There was no way Shane would interrupt her on an undercover assignment if his world wasn't crumbling.

"I was about to ask you the same question," he stated, sounding a little offended.

"I can't really talk right now but I'm fine if that's what you're asking," she said, confused by how cautious he was being.

"Good to know because Preston called—"

"Hold on right there," she said. "I'm not having this discussion with you, Shane. You're my brother and I love you but this is out of bounds and completely inappropriate under the circumstances."

"Well. I just—"

"Didn't think?" She finished his sentence for him, steaming mad.

One of the kiddos screamed bloody murder in the background.

"You should go take care of that, Shane," she said, leaving no room for doubt as to where she stood on this topic. "Your kids need you more than I do right now."

"Got it," he said. She hoped it was true, because she had no plans to discuss someone she was dating or not dating with her family. If Preston couldn't keep their relationship between the two of them she had no plans to return his texts.

"Bye," she said before ending the call. Her auburn hair had always been blamed for her fiery temper, but her brothers sure knew how to push her buttons. They were probably more to blame for her short fuse than a genetic trait.

Ree took a couple of minutes to walk off her anger before returning to the bar. The minute she stepped inside, she caught sight of the waitress talking to Quint. The woman twirled her hair around her finger, a sure sign of flirting.

A few calming breaths later, Ree was ready to face her second frustration in fifteen minutes. The way this date night was going she'd be home in bed alone by nine thirty. Okay, the thought made Ree giggle and lightened some of her frustration. She really was going all in emotionally with the fake marriage. Good. She needed to be invested in order to sell the relationship.

"Hey, sorry about that," she said as she walked up to her "husband" and the waitress. She stopped beside Quint and wrapped her arms around his neck before planting a mind-blowing kiss on his lips. "My brother can be dramatic."

"Everything okay with your mom? I was just telling Kelsey about your mom's fall," he said.

"Yes, she's doing much better." She had no idea what he was talking about, so she just went with it.

"I'm still impressed she decided to get on the ladder at her age to clean out gutters," he said, subtly bringing her up to speed.

"My mom is the original DIY lady," she quipped, smiling at Kelsey.

"Are y'all newlyweds?" Kelsey asked.

"How did you know?" Ree asked.

"Shiny bands," she quipped. "Plus, y'all are way too adorable holding hands and cuddling up to each other to be old-timers."

"Guilty," Ree stated.

"How did the two of you meet?" Kelsey continued.

"A pizza place in Austin," she said and then instantly realized that was their first-date story. Her cheeks might have given her away as a red blush crawled up her neck, the glow so bright she could probably land planes if she stood beside a runway. She could only pray the dimly lit room would provide camouflage.

"Actually, that was our first date, honey," Quint said to cover her mistake. "We met at Tony's New Year's Eve party."

"I just totally heard that wrong," Ree stated. "Duh." She made a show of smacking herself on the forehead. "I've literally been working way too many hours lately."

The waitress laughed. She also seemed to know when to make an exit because she excused herself to go check on another table.

"Great job with the jealousy act earlier," Quint whispered into her ear.

"Not so much on the first-date story," she pointed out.

"Don't beat yourself up. We didn't rehearse that one," he said but she couldn't let herself off the hook so easily.

However, with his lips this close, his warm breath on her neck, all kinds of sensations skittered across her skin. Her body became keenly aware of his as he looped an arm around her waist and hauled her against him. He positioned her on his lap and held onto her, resting his hand on her back for a long moment.

If only the jealousy bit was an act. Unfortunately, she wasn't that good an actress.

Her reaction also made her rethink responding to Preston's text. Had she opened a hornet's nest in responding to the first one?

With Quint's arms around her, holding her, all thoughts of another man dissolved. She breathed in his spicy male scent, allowing all that was Quint to fill her senses. It would be so easy to fall for this man hook, line and sinker.

If only they hadn't met on the job, she thought. But then, that might not matter. He was hurting and leaning into her for support. His emotions were running high and he was channeling them into her right now. The intensity she felt was for his loss and not because he couldn't live without her. The way he made her feel like she was the only woman in the world right now didn't mean there was anything real going on between them. He had to sell the relationship as much as she did. He was clearly doing his part, because a piece of her was starting to believe he'd fallen head over heels in love with her.

How was that for good acting on his part?

The feeling of eyes on her shifted Ree's attention. The hairs on the back of her neck prickled. Was someone watching them?

Chapter Sixteen

"What is it?" Quint asked Ree. He felt her body suddenly stiffen. Every one of her muscles tensed.

She turned enough to whisper in his ear. "Someone's watching us. I can feel it."

"Okay." He feathered a few kisses on her neck, creating an intimate scene for onlookers. Most would redirect their gazes at the public display of affection. Folks became awkward real fast when lovers crossed a line, became too intimate.

With hooded eyes, he scanned as much of the room as he could see from his vantage point. The little moans of pleasure escaping Ree's lips when he shifted in his seat or moved his hands weren't helping him concentrate.

Clearly, he was distracted. He blamed it on the heavy emotions from dredging up the past. There were times when he thought the hole in his heart could never be filled. He certainly didn't deserve to be happy when Tessa couldn't. He didn't deserve to keep doing the job he loved when she couldn't.

And he sure as hell didn't deserve to be in love with someone when she couldn't.

How was that for messed-up?

The irony was that he knew, in his heart of hearts, that Tessa would never want him to be unhappy. If she was here, she would be the first one to punch him in the arm and tell him to get over it already. Guilt and shame for letting her down would cloak him for the rest of his life.

Oddly, when he was with Ree, the pain wasn't so great that he couldn't handle it. In fact, it was the first time since the ordeal happened six months ago that he felt a small sense of relief.

"Do you have a visual?" he asked when he couldn't find anyone in the crowd staring at them. The crowd was thickening by the minute as the band kicked off their first song.

"No. It's strange, though, because I could have sworn someone was locked onto us," she admitted, casually casing the room. "Maybe behind us?"

"It's definitely not cool to be caught checking everyone out when we're supposed to only have eyes for each other," he stated. "Don't worry about it. We'll stick around for a while. See if anything comes up."

He could tell she was being too hard on herself when she felt like she missed something, and he respected her for it. It meant she cared a whole helluva lot about what she was doing. Sometimes, the passion could become misguided and a person could become too critical of themselves. Always pushing.

Never giving themselves a well-deserved break. Constantly playing out scenarios in their minds when they should be sleeping.

No one operated well under such internal scrutiny. He should know. It was his past.

Was he doing it again? This time with Tessa's death?

He had been over and over the scenario in his mind dozens of times. What could he have done differently? Of course, the most obvious was that he could have stopped her from being there altogether. That was the one his mind kept snapping back to. But on the scene, he should have intervened and stopped her from going inside the building. Of course, that would mean she would have to explain why her partner suddenly didn't think she was fit to go inside like everyone else.

Tessa had given him those eyes that had been so good at communicating to him. They begged him to stop and let her do her job one more time. She'd already said once she became a desk jockey she would always be a desk jockey. Having a kid meant she would change her life. Having the kid on her own meant she needed to insure she would be coming home every night.

Tessa had never stressed about the dangers of the job in the past. She'd been changing before his eyes. He understood, approved even. But dammit, she should have come home that night instead of him.

Before he got too worked up over Tessa, he shifted his focus to Ree.

"I'm going to go sit in my chair now," she said as though she'd been party to the mental discussion he'd just had.

"It'll be good to have us facing opposite directions," he said with very little enthusiasm. The truth was that he liked holding her in his arms. He liked the feel of her heartbeat against his body. And he liked how well she fit him. This seemed like a good time to remind himself they weren't there to bond. He condemned himself once again for losing focus. If he'd been paying closer attention, he might have a description of the person who'd been watching them by now.

Ree moved across the table from him and casually picked up her beer. She glanced around as she started grooving to the beat. Her face was unreadable as to whether or not she was having the same physical reaction to Quint that he was having to her. He needed to know if her judgment was being affected. At least, that was what he told himself.

Setting her beer down, she smiled at Quint. It had the same effect as the sun burning through clouds, warming everything it touched with beams of light.

Quint couldn't help but crack a smile over that one. Since when did he become a poet?

"Did you still want to try the mechanical bull?" he asked when he realized she couldn't find anyone staring at them.

"I'd puke," she said, rubbing her stomach. "I can barely fit any of this beer in."

He had to laugh at her honesty. The beers were mostly for show. Neither would finish theirs.

"I doubt you'll need dessert tonight," he quipped, thinking there were a whole lot of other things he'd like to do instead but couldn't.

She groaned before diverting her gaze, locking onto someone across the room. "It's probably nothing but I've seen one of the guys over there at the restaurant."

"Small towns can be like that," he said.

She pulled lipstick and her phone out of her handbag.

"What are you planning to do with those things?" he asked, curious as to how those items went together.

"Watch and learn," she said with a smirk. She uncapped the lipstick. Held her cell phone up. "Selfie mode turns this guy into a mirror." She applied two coats of a deep red lipstick before pressing her lips together. "We can compare notes later."

It dawned on him that she'd just snapped pictures of the guy in question.

"I know it's still early, but I'm beat from the last few days at work," she said. "Do you want to go home?"

Quint couldn't get to his feet fast enough. There hadn't been anything to see so far, and after watching Kelsey bolt around, he could only imagine how exhausting waiting tables must be for Ree. An iPad that had been attached to the table allowed him to pull up his check and then pay without signaling for the waitress.

Within minutes the two were headed out the door.

Quint noticed a male standing near the exit. He had on a red flannel shirt with cutoff sleeves, a pair of jeans and a white Stetson. The man was probably five feet ten inches if Quint had to guess. The reason he wore cutoff sleeves was to show off the arm muscles of a lumberjack. Last time Quint checked, Texas had more cattle ranches than lumberyards. Quint shrugged. The guy looked familiar, though. Maybe going home to look at footage would help place him. Or not. The name came to Quint. The guy was Phillip.

"WHAT WAS PHILLIP doing there?" Ree couldn't stop thinking about the man in the flannel shirt on the way home. There wasn't much in the way of conversation between her and Quint. They were inching along, making progress. Quint now had an in at Greenlight, working on the computer. She was making ground on her relationships with Chef and Adrian. Fender was still a mystery. She hadn't quite figured Charley out yet. And Zoey, that poor young woman, weighed heavily on Ree's mind.

"Your guess is as good as mine," Quint said.

"Are you thinking what I am? He is the one responsible for paying the maid to spy on us?" she asked.

"I'd be lying if I said it didn't cross my mind," he stated.

"Should we turn around and follow him?" She craned her neck around.

"There's no need. He's been behind me for the

past three miles," Quint stated. "If we had turned back, we would have played right into his hands. Our cover would have been blown. He looked me dead in the eyes when we walked out." Quint pulled into the parking spot in front of the cabin as the vehicle behind them drove on past. Greenlight seemed to be rockin' and rollin'. Relief washed over her that she didn't have to work tonight. As busy as she'd been over the past few days, she wasn't sure her feet could handle another shift.

A loud voice carried across the parking lot as they exited the sedan. She shot Quint a glance. He nodded. She recognized the voice as Adrian's.

Moving purposefully, they rounded the dark side of the cabin that faced the street. The voice wasn't coming from the parking lot; it came from behind the restaurant. There was a second voice, too. Fender's.

Ree strained to make out the details of what they were saying. She pulled out her cell phone and hit the video button to try to get some kind of recording that could be sent to the lab later. She glanced around, thinking they needed to get closer. Quint was already taking action.

There was a gaggle of trees toward the back of the parking lot, separating the other cabins from Greenlight. The trees also acted as a sound barrier. Quint made eye contact as he eased toward the first tree.

It was a huge risk, but this could be the turning point they so desperately needed in the investigation. Then again, they might end up witnessing nothing more than a lover's quarrel. But Fender and Adrian?

Ree had to really think about that one. A relationship could explain why Adrian had been so secretive
and never wanted to talk about anything that went on
at Greenlight. It could also explain why she seemed
to be so protective of the kitchen. Were there other
signs Ree had missed? Would a more experienced
agent have seen the signs?

Before she had a chance to work herself up to a
point of no return, she followed Quint. Tree by tree,
they pushed closer as the pair of voices shot across
the lot. It sounded like an argument, from the tone
of the exchange. Again, Ree's mind snapped back
to the thought they were lovers. Again, she tried to
discount the possibility.

Keeping an open mind was the hallmark of a great
investigator. It would stop her from missing important details. Removing personal bias out of an investigation could be tricky. Mentally taking a step
back to allow the facts to speak for themselves and
not locking onto an opinion too early would allow
the truth to bubble up to the surface.

She held her phone toward the quarrelers, hoping
the sound quality would be good enough for the lab
to analyze. This was definitely the time she wished
she had a booster with her. They'd had to keep equipment to a minimum in the event Charley had con-
nections to the owners of the cabin. Small towns had
their charms and one of them was people tended to
know each other. If there was a connection and a
favor was called in, the cabin needed to be as clean
as possible. Even the laptop's screen saving pass-

word was encrypted. The only information someone could get out of "hacking" into his laptop would be exactly what the government agency wanted them to reveal—a fake screen set up by a genius tech agent. The person would be privy to a fake email account set up as Quint's, and a desktop with links to a convincing but fake online computer degree program that appeared to be in process.

Ree strained to hear but couldn't make out the words. Quint's movements were impressive, to say the least. The man was stealth whereas she felt loud. Even his footsteps were silent, not a single crunch. He seemed to feel his way with calm, deliberate steps. She chalked it up to his years of practice and experience.

A door slammed. A curse was shouted. And then the sound of a motorcycle engine roaring to life ripped through the night. Fender took off, spewing gravel underneath his tires. This had all the signs of a lovers' fight.

But Ree decided not to snap to judgment too quickly. She challenged herself to think about what else it might be as Quint linked their fingers and they made their way back to the cabin, careful not to draw attention.

Once safely inside, she huddled up with Quint and played back the video.

"The music is too loud in the background. The way sound carries, I couldn't get a recording that is discernible to the naked ear," she said on a frustrated sigh.

Quint stood there not two feet away from her. His arms were folded over his chest and his head bowed as he listened intently. "No, but I saw you reach for your phone the minute you heard voices. Your instincts are spot-on. It's why I didn't need to reach for mine. I saw what you were doing."

His reassurance helped but her frustration was still high at her mistakes.

"You probably already realized you can send this off to the lab for analysis," he continued when she didn't respond. "And you're right. They have pulled off some miracles. We can upload the video right now and get its place in line for analysis. Grappell can manage the process for us from there."

She gave a slight nod at that.

Quint walked over to his laptop and booted it up. An alert filled the screen after he entered his password.

"Someone has been in the cabin," he said.

Ree couldn't get beside him fast enough. She perched on the edge of the couch, sitting so close their thighs touched. She'd grown accustomed to the electric current that came with contact. Anticipated it. Needed it?

Pushing the thought aside, she stared at the access warning that filled the screen. When someone besides Quint tried to access the computer, a picture was taken.

Quint's fingers danced across the keyboard.

"Zoey?" she said. "What on earth would she be doing here trying to get into the computer?"

Quint seemed to be thinking long and hard. "If the abuse theory holds water, she might have gotten in a fight with her boyfriend or been kicked out of the motel where she was staying."

"We make good tips," Ree countered. "Why wouldn't she have enough money to pay for a place?"

"Her boyfriend could have rented it," he offered. "If he left her high and dry, she might not have another place to go."

"You changed the locks." Ree's eyes widened. She glanced around. There weren't a whole lot of places to hide in this small cabin. She held a finger up before popping to her feet. Not three minutes later, they cleared the place before proceeding. Thankfully, Zoey wasn't there, or she would have overheard too much.

"A good skeleton key would work on what I bought from the hardware store," he supplied.

"Seems like Zoey has many talents. I can't help but wonder if she's involved with Phillip in some way." Ree moved to the fridge. Opening the door, she instantly noticed food was gone. "Wasn't there some milk left in the carton?"

"There should be. I didn't drink it," he said.

Ree glanced at the trash under the sink. The carton was there.

"The cheese is missing too," she noticed. There were other things gone—a pair of apples, lunch meat and half the lettuce. "Maybe your theory is right after all. She must be hungry, but I wonder what's happening to her money. We both know that I make more than enough to cover food and put a roof over our heads."

"She might have been robbed. A guy she was dating could have taken her money and disappeared. It might have been the reason she wanted to change shifts with you," he offered. "I'm reaching here."

Ree nodded. "I saw a huge bruise on her arm. She's withdrawn, doesn't really speak to Adrian or me."

"It's impossible to know what's going on without digging into her circumstances a little more," he continued. "She might have any number of addiction issues."

Again, she agreed.

"There could be a relative in the background needing the money," he surmised.

"Something is bothering me and I can't quite pinpoint what it is," she admitted.

He nodded. "Hold on to it, because intuition is usually right when backed by training and experience."

She had all kinds of intuition and plenty of training, but not a good handle on Zoey. Confronting her at work tomorrow might get the answers Ree was searching for.

Chapter Seventeen

Quint woke early and checked his email. He realized it was too soon to get analysis back on the images he'd been sending over to Grappell, but he hoped. There was nothing.

He did, however, have an email from his boss. *How's the case?*

Not yet ready to respond, he drained his coffee cup and closed his laptop. There was a problem with the two of them sleeping in separate beds now that they'd picked up a snoop. He remade the couch and slid his pillow onto Ree's bed.

Her steady, even breathing said she was still in a deep sleep. The urge to climb under the covers next to her and draw her close caught him off guard. He couldn't walk away fast enough. Outside, the temperature was already warm, the sun hot, as he locked the door and crossed the parking lot.

A question from last night bugged him. How did Zoey get inside their cabin? Then again, security wasn't exactly tight here. Thankfully, he'd hid the tackle box behind the washer/dryer combo in the hall closet. His next step would be to find out her last name and have Grappell run a background check. Of course, Zoey might not even be her real first name. So many questions with that one. Could he get a fingerprint and have Grappell run it through the database? It would work if she had a driver's license or even a criminal record.

Moving on from Zoey, he was still chewing on the disagreement between Adrian and Fender last night. Since Quint was coming in mornings, he hadn't had a chance to work the relationship he'd started developing with Stevie the bartender.

Then, there was the fight between Charley and his cousin. Tensions seemed to be running high at Greenlight. Where there was smoke, there usually was fire. There was enough to indicate a forest fire around here. Smoke everywhere. No flame.

The door to the restaurant was unlocked, so Quint walked inside. Rather than call out, he headed to the back and to the small office. No one was around, which was surprising. There was an SUV parked out front alongside Charley's truck. Quint had memorized the license plate. He pulled out his cell and sent the plate information to Grappell.

A loud banging noise caught his attention as he moved the mouse to wake up the desktop computer. Instinct and adrenaline had Quint on his feet in two seconds. He reminded himself about the boot he was wearing so he wouldn't give himself away in the heat of the moment.

More noise came from the opposite hallway leading toward the bathroom.

"Everything okay out there?" he shouted from the office. In times like these, he also had to remind himself that he was supposed to be a regular Joe Schmo, and not a highly trained agent with a black belt in kung fu.

There was a loud grunt, followed by the sound of someone being thrown against the wall. The noise got Quint moving in its direction. It appeared as if someone was being killed and he couldn't stand by and listen without trying to do something about it.

As he rounded the corner of the hallway, he saw Charley straightening his shirt. The metal side door was closing.

"Everything okay?" Quint asked.

"Me? I'm fine. Just had a skirmish with someone I kicked out last night. He thought he left his wallet here and didn't believe me when I said no one had turned it in." Charley kept his face down but when it turned toward Quint, it was easy to see the man's nose was bleeding.

"Your nose," Quint said, but Charley waved him off.

"It's okay. All over now," Charley said.

"Are you sure about that?" Quint needed to push back a little. "I'm here to help. I can call the deputy or—"

"No. No. Slight misunderstanding is all. No crime has been committed here." Charley gave a forced smile. "Why don't you go on back to the office and finish whatever it is that you were working on. There's no trouble."

"You sure about that?" Quint asked.

"One hundred percent," Charley assured him. "Chef is going to be here in a few minutes. I need to make room for a delivery."

Quint made a show of being reluctant about leaving. Charley made eyes that told Quint to retreat. So he did. The camera back at home would be recording the SUV and driver as they exited. Quint had a plate. Before he could forget any important details and while Charley was still in the hallway, Quint shot a quick note to Grappell with everything he could remember about the exchange and the mystery guest.

Tensions at Greenlight were most definitely a boiling pot on a hot stove.

An hour later, Quint came home and updated Ree on the morning's events before letting her know that he'd planted an app on the desktop that would give him remote access without anyone being the wiser. Before he could get into much else with her, she walked out the door for work.

"I THOUGHT YOU might want to use this next time." Ree walked over to Zoey's station before their shift began and set a key down on the table.

Zoey blanched, her skin paled, and then she quickly covered by clearing her throat. She shrugged, trying to look casual and failing miserably. "I don't know what you're talking about."

"It's okay. I'm not mad and neither is Quint," she

said in the same tone of voice she would use if she was talking about picking up the mail. Consistency was key. Calmness was key. Understanding was key.

"Why should you be?" she quipped, finding some of her usual sass.

"I'm not." Ree pulled a piece of paper and pen out of her apron. She set those on the same table, moving the key on top. "In fact, why don't you just write down a few of your favorites from the grocery store so I can make sure they're stocked in the house next time."

"There won't be a next time because there wasn't a first." Zoey's tone was defiant and she came off more than a little embarrassed.

Ree was convinced more than ever that Zoey was in some kind of abusive relationship. Since pushing the issue would be a whole lot like cornering a wounded animal, Ree turned around and walked off. To do otherwise could prove dangerous and naive. Besides, Ree had put it out there. Zoey now knew they were on to her and she had to be wondering how they knew. There'd been no judgment about the incident. Only understanding and a not-so-subtle offer of help.

The other incident from last night could be nothing more than a lovers' fight. In fact, what else could it be?

Besides, how many eligible men and women were there in a small town? It was exactly the reason Ree had dated friends of her brothers growing up, and look where that had gotten her. She'd learned real quickly that her brothers were way too in the know about her personal life when it all became intertwined. Shane's call last night still struck a raw nerve.

Adrian blew through without saying a whole lot. Fine by Ree. She wasn't in the mood to speak to someone who lied to her. Betrayed her? At the very least kept secrets from her.

Adrian and Ree weren't friends in real life. Why did the relationship with Fender rub her the wrong way? Adrian could date anyone she wanted.

Sure, the woman was secretive. She didn't gossip at work. Those were probably signs that she was up to something. The fact she knew Zoey might be young and in a relationship that could hurt her but was unwilling to do anything about it also didn't sit well with Ree.

Then again, maybe she woke up on the wrong side of the bed today. She closed her eyes with her mind churning and woke in the same spin cycle. She still couldn't pinpoint what it was about Adrian and Fender's relationship that bugged her so much. Was it that the relationship was happening right underneath her nose and she hadn't caught onto it? Had she made another critical mistake?

Although with all of Quint's experience, he hadn't caught on to it, either. Then again, he wasn't the one working with Adrian. He probably would have been able to handle waiting tables, working the other waitstaff, the kitchen, all while gathering intel. He would probably be on top of everything.

Ree needed a nap. She was cranky as all get-out.

Exhaustion wore her thin after tossing and turning most of the night. She'd finally fallen asleep as the sun came up. Ree needed her sleep, too. Maybe another cup of coffee would do the trick.

She walked into the kitchen as the first customer walked through the front door. From behind her, she heard Zoey greet them and ask if they preferred a table or booth. At least Ree was back to working one shift a day. She could get through a lunch rush.

"What's wrong with you today?" Adrian asked, surprising Ree from behind.

She jumped and clutched at her heart. She should probably be acting at this point but Adrian had actually caught Ree off guard.

"Guy trouble?" Adrian asked, taking a cup from the counter.

"Tired," Ree admitted. At least she could be honest about that one aspect of her life.

"Perk up," Adrian teased with an elbow jab to the rib cage. "It's gonna be a busy one today."

"What about you? Any guy problems lately?" Ree asked Adrian.

"Isn't there always?" Adrian shrugged, trying a little too hard to be nonchalant.

After finishing the first cup of coffee, Ree didn't have five seconds to catch her breath for the next few hours. The nice part was the day zipped by and she got into a decent rhythm waiting on customers. If this whole law enforcement thing didn't work out, she could waitress for a living. Lack of sleep was really getting to her now. She was making corny jokes. Worse yet, they were to herself.

Zoey passed by Ree and stuffed something in Ree's pocket.

"Don't look at it now," Zoey demanded.

As she was on her way out, one of the barmaids checked in. She was here early. Ree took note of the bleached blonde with a tan and legs for days.

"Hey," Ree said as they passed each other.

The blonde didn't give her the time of day as she rushed past, heading toward the kitchen door where Charley waited with a scowl on his face. Ree thought about Adrian and Fender's argument last night. She made a mental note to watch their interactions over the next couple of days.

Middle of July in Texas meant walking back to the cabin in pavement-melting heat. Quint waited at the door, as usual, and Adrian winked at Ree as she left. What was Adrian so happy about? Based on her fight with Fender last night, she was a screaming mess. Had Ree misjudged the situation? Had Adrian brought him outside to reem Fender out for something work-related? He was the expeditor, after all. It was his job to keep the work flowing and meals delivered fresh and hot.

Ree filed the information in the back of her mind and moved on.

"I need a cool shower and ice packs for my tired feet," Ree stated as she walked in the door. She reached in her apron to empty her pocket when she realized Zoey's note was inside.

Ree walked to the table after toeing off her boots. She smoothed out the crinkled-up piece of paper and read the list: Cap'n Crunch Berries, apples, cheese swirls, bread, lunch meat and milk. The word *lettuce* had been hastily scribbled at the bottom.

A tear welled in Ree's eyes. This wasn't the grocery list of a grown adult. This was the grocery list of a college-age kid.

Quint walked over, stopping beside her. Ree ducked her head, chin to chest, to hide the rogue tear that fell, staining the slip of paper.

He didn't speak. Instead, he wrapped an arm around her. She turned into his muscled chest and cried.

"It's okay," he said, whispering other reassurances in her ear. "We'll get help for her. She's not alone any longer. She has us."

As crazy as Ree's childhood might have been after she lost her father at a young age, Ree wouldn't change a thing except for maybe bringing him back. She had few memories of the man before he died. Her grandfather and brothers had provided more than enough male influences in her life. She couldn't imagine her life without them despite needing breathing room.

Were they annoying at times? Yes. Did they cross boundaries that shouldn't be crossed? Yes. Did they also have hearts of gold and ultimately want what was best for her? Absolutely yes.

She made a mental note to circle back after this

case was over and tell Shane that he still needed to stay out of her business, but she loved him anyway.

As for Quint? It was difficult not to start falling for a guy who seemed to know when to pull her into a hug and when to give her space. This assignment, this "act" of being married to this amazing man was getting inside her head. Was that part of what had kept her awake last night?

To be honest, yes. She'd drifted in and out of sleep alternating between thinking about the case, and how incredible it had felt to be in Quint's arms. One thing was clear: she couldn't fall for a coworker. Not only would that be unprofessional, but it could distract her at a critical moment as well. She needed to get her head back in the arena. She needed to face reality. Quint was temporary. Once this assignment was over, the two of them would be saying goodbye.

It was a harsh truth. One she needed to accept in order to move on with her life.

Chapter Eighteen

It was true. A good night of sleep could cure almost anything. Ree stretched her arms out wide and yawned. Quint's bed was made back into a couch. His pillow was on hers. He must still be next door at Greenlight.

She threw off her covers, pushed out of bed and headed toward the coffeepot. It was already brewed. All she could think was that she could get used to this treatment.

At thirty-six, was it time to think about settling down? Ree had no idea where these thoughts were coming from. She'd never been the type to depend on someone else. And yet, sharing this cabin was making her realize there might be more to life than her job.

Gasp.

Was that true? Could she begin to consider a life that didn't involve thinking about work 24/7? She'd worked so hard to get where she was and still had a lot of track left in front of her. The thought of trying to balance both had never really held much appeal.

But she could admit that lately she'd felt a certain sense of loneliness about her life. She'd been attributing it to burnout, figuring a good vacation would do the trick and get her back in the game.

She pulled up her fake social media account as she nursed her cup of coffee. The images of her and Quint from the night before last, looking so happy but also knowing it was so fake, hit her square in the chest. A hot tear rolled down her cheek and a hollow feeling ripped through her chest.

The reaction couldn't be about Quint. She'd only known him less than a week. Although, to be fair, it felt much longer.

Ree wasn't ready to unpack the real reason. Instead, she flattened out the slip of paper from Zoey, careful to straighten out the edges. Ree couldn't always bring justice or right wrongs in her job. More often than not, she was able to lock a bad guy away. But there were times to take a stand, go above and beyond. For the next hour, she researched services for women in abusive relationships.

There was something very right about how this path made her feel. As cliché as it might sound, she'd gotten into law enforcement to make a difference.

Ree made breakfast, finished a second cup of coffee and dressed. Greenlight closed at three o'clock on Sundays after what she'd been told at one point on her shift yesterday would be a legendary brunch.

She clocked in early, passing Quint in the parking lot on the way over.

He hauled her against his chest before whispering, "We have another break in the case. Tell you all about it later."

He pulled his head back, gazed into her eyes and then pressed a kiss to her lips. She brought her hands up to his face, deepening the kiss. He tasted like French roast coffee and bacon. Her new favorite combination.

"See you at home later," he stated with a look that made her think she'd caught him off guard.

"Can't wait to finish this shift," she said. Before heading to the restaurant, she added, "I missed you this morning."

Her comment clearly caught him off guard. He recovered quickly. "Me, too."

"One more thing," she said before she let him go. "I left Zoey's list on the table. Would you mind running to the store and bringing the items with you when you come to walk me home later?"

"I'd be more than happy to," he stated with conviction.

"Thank you." She smiled at him. Really smiled. Not the fake wife smile but one that came from the heart.

Sunday brunch had a different setup than the rest of the week. The whole shebang was arranged as a buffet with various stations, one of which was a Belgian waffle station. The cooks were out, ready to man their stations. Cars started filling the parking lot in anticipation of opening.

"What's going on today?" she asked Adrian.

"The good news is that we're done by three o'clock,"

Adrian said. "The bad news is if you think we were busy before, you haven't met Sunday brunch."

"Sounds scary." Ree could hardly imagine being busier.

"Basically," Adrian went on, "you won't need to exercise for a week. It's constant running to clear plates, attend to drinks. Charley wants coffee mugs refilled at all times. Word of warning. He doesn't like it when customers have to ask for service."

Ree searched her memory to see if she'd been attentive enough to her customers. She couldn't recall any needing to flag her down, so that had to be a good sign. "Okay. Good to know. Anything else?"

Adrian motioned toward the line already forming at the door. "Strap on your seat belt. You're in for one wild ride."

Within minutes, the room filled with customers, the running started and didn't stop until half past three, when the last of the customers cashed out. Ree took one look at Adrian, who was sitting down, propping up her head with her hands.

"Told you so," was all Adrian said as Ree texted Quint.

"I'm not sure that was adequate warning for what just happened," Ree joked.

"Money's good, though." Adrian rubbed the tips of her fingers together with her thumb.

Fender cut through the dining room and Adrian's smile dropped so hard it could have hit the floor.

"Everything all right between the two of you?" Ree asked.

"Of course. Why do you ask?" Adrian seemed caught off guard by the question.

"I've got eyes," Ree shot back. "And I'm not stupid."

Adrian shot a warning look. "Well, you better keep those eyes closed and your mouth shut if you want to get along."

With that, Adrian stormed off and made it more than clear she was done talking to Ree.

By the time Ree closed out her station, Quint stood at the door. She walked to him and he hauled her to his chest. She was going to miss the intensity of his touch and the way her heart danced every time she saw him. He discreetly handed her a bag of groceries, which she held out behind her as Zoey left the building.

"Thanks," Zoey murmured, taking the offering before heading down the road on foot. She did a great job of hiding the bag in front of her as she disappeared.

Ree remembered what Quint had told her the last time he hugged her in the parking lot. There was a development in the case. In a couple of minutes, she was going to find out if it was the break they needed.

QUINT CLOSED AND locked the door behind them back at the cabin.

"I asked Adrian about Fender," she started.

"And?"

"It didn't go well," Ree said on a sigh.

"What happened here today?" Ree asked as she

headed toward the closet. "Please talk away but I have to get out of this uniform."

Did she have to go and put the mental image of her stripping off her clothes in his mind?

Quint performed a mental headshake. "There was someone at Greenlight this morning. He gave Charley a bloody nose by the bathrooms. I went over to check on the commotion and he was gone. I did think to get a license plate on the way in."

"Sounds promising," she shouted from down the hall.

He moved to the fridge and opened a bottle of Coke for her. He set it on the table along with the tray of meats, cheeses and fruits that he'd picked up at the grocery during his store run.

"He kept his face down for the camera, so we didn't get a good image there like I'd hoped to," he explained. "However, Grappell is running the plate through the database to see if he can get a hit."

"That's encouraging," she said, reemerging wearing form-hugging exercise pants and a soft cotton tee. Ree could make a paper bag look sexy. "What did Charley say?"

"That it was no big deal. There certainly has been a lot of activity at Greenlight. I installed spyware on Charley's desktop. Fingers crossed there," he continued.

"Charley doesn't seem like the type to put up with being hit," she stated.

"Not to me, either. Not unless he has to," Quint said.

Ree stopped at the table. "Holy smokes. What is all this?"

"Food. Something to drink. Your feet must be ready to fall off after a week at Greenlight," he teased.

"I don't know how anyone does it. How do they keep running around? I'm ready to drop." She took a seat and started right in. "Thank you for this, by the way."

He waved her off. She didn't need to thank him. It was teamwork as far as he was concerned.

"It is a big deal to me," she said, making eyes at him. "You know, for someone who never wants to get married you sure would make an amazing husband."

He didn't know what to do with that statement, so he let it sit there between them.

"I wasn't suggesting you should get married or anything," she said as if anxious to clarify. "In fact, your marital status is none of my business." The way the words came out in a rush, practically tripping all over each other, he could tell she spoke before she thought.

"Don't worry. I'm not offended," he stated for the record, adding, "Marriage probably works for some people. I don't have anything against the institution in and of itself. It's not for everyone."

"Can I ask you a personal question?" She didn't bring her eyes up to meet his. Instead, she twirled a piece of cheese between her fingers.

"Go for it," he said.

"You're obviously very dedicated to your job. It

shows. You probably already know this but you are kind of a legend at the agency," she began.

So far, he didn't see a question.

"Do you ever find yourself in a spot where you're just flat-out lonely? Like, it might be nice to share your day with someone special or feel as if you can take off your gun and badge, and relax with your girl, or in my case, guy?" she asked.

There was a lot to unpack in her statement turned questions.

"Let's see if I understand what you're asking," he started and she slowly brought her gaze up to meet his. "Do I ever get lonely?"

She nodded.

"I didn't used to. Since losing my best friend and partner, the answer is yes. All the time." He surprised himself with the admission. "Does that mean I would change being focused on my career...the answer there is no. I can't imagine doing anything else in life."

His last statement was partially true. After losing Tessa, he had thrown himself deeper into his career. Recently, he'd questioned if there was anything else he might want to do for a living. He'd dabbled with a few thoughts of retiring from the agency and starting a small business like a bait shop where he could live next to a lake.

But that was only recently.

"If you ever wanted to leave this career behind, you could totally start a food truck business," she stated. "You're very good at feeding people."

He chuckled. "I don't know how good I'd be at that, but I'll take the compliment."

"You should consider it once you're done with undercover work," she said with a bright smile. "Oh, actually, with those muscles you could be a trainer."

Her cheeks flamed with the admission.

"I'm pretty sure that's already happening," he quipped with a wink.

"Well, yeah, there is that," she said. "I highly doubt you're going to be stuck with me through another assignment. I'm half surprised you didn't already kick me back after our dicey start."

He shot her a look.

"How many times have you thought about quitting since you started this line of work?" he asked.

"Me?" She looked him square in the eye. "None."

"Then, you might just make it to retirement," he stated.

"The only guy I've dated seriously in years thought I was too focused on work to be in a relationship," she said. "He asked me to reevaluate my priorities."

"What did you do?" he asked, not really wanting to hear about her relationship with another man even though he had no designs on her.

"I did as he asked," she said. "It led me to break up with him."

"And now?" he asked.

"I don't know. Sometimes I question whether or not I've done the right thing by always putting my personal life behind my career. I wonder if I'll end up with a bunch of accolades and no one to share the news with. You know?" She cocked an eyebrow as she tossed a piece of cheese back onto the tray.

"As a matter of fact, I do," he admitted. "The choices I've made are obvious."

"You can't become the best at something if you only give it half your attention," she said.

"That was always my philosophy," he stated. "But then, I also had Tessa to fill in the gap."

"And now?" She turned his question back on him.

"Life can be a real face punch," he said, wishing he could go back for five minutes and tell Tessa how much she meant to him. His cell buzzed, indicating an email had come in. "Grappell might have gotten a hit. I should check this."

Chapter Nineteen

"What is it?" Ree asked, letting his statement about life sit in the back of her mind as she watched him check his phone.

He moved over to the laptop and then brought it over to the table. She cleared off space and then moved her chair beside his, ignoring the heat washing over her body at being so close. "Grappell got a hit on the plate."

Bald Guy. "It's registered to an eighty-year-old female by the name of Betsy Warner. She lives about an hour away from here," he informed. "Grappell attached the address with a map pinpointing the location."

"I'm guessing the agency is sending someone else to follow up on the lead," she said.

He nodded. "No one wants to risk us being seen or made. Grappell said he'd keep us posted on what they find out."

More waiting around. *Great.*

"In the meantime, we can go through last night's footage to see what else we can dig up," he suggested, rubbing his hands together. "It's not the sexiest part of the job but it is where most of the work is done."

"Remind me not to sign up for any more possible long-term undercover gigs unless it's with you," she said in response. "At least your food game is strong."

"I see the SUV parked again on Thursday," he said as he studied the screen with a slight smirk.

"How badly do you want to go check out the house it's registered to?" she asked.

"As much as I want to breathe air," he stated.

"Remind me how wrong it would be for us to take a drive right now," she said.

"And give Grappell an ulcer?" he shot back with a grin that said he could easily be talked into it.

She wiggled her eyebrows. And then the thing that had been niggling at the back of her mind at the bar last night stepped out of the shadows.

"He was at the bar," she said.

"Who?" He arched a dark brow.

"Bald Guy. We were focused on Phillip but Bald Guy was standing next to him. The guy from the sketch. He was there and I'm certain the two of them were together."

She grabbed her phone and located the picture she'd taken.

"Yes. See. He's right here," she said, holding up her cell so he could get a good look.

"That's him," Quint confirmed. "Before we decide to go for a drive, I need to dig around in Charley's files. See what I can come up with."

The minute Quint located evidence, Charley would be arrested, and the assignment would come to a close. The thought shouldn't make her heart hurt. Once arrests were made, she wouldn't be able to show her face and Zoey would continue to be left to her own devices. Without this job, what would she do for money? Would conditions worsen for her?

"Bingo," Quint said. "I'm seeing a lot of money come through here and into a bank that we know is fake. This is tens of thousands of dollars a day. He is breaking up large amounts of money into smaller transactions, shuffling through this fake account and into his business account. From there it's going into untraceable shell companies."

"Does that mean he isn't moving weapons?" she asked.

"It could be where the money is coming from but I'm not seeing any evidence of guns moving out the back door. Let me send a note to Grappell with this new information. He's going to want to give tech a few days to take a deep dive into this and put together the case. I'll update the boss, too. She'll want to identify who the shell accounts belong to so they can bust as many people as possible," he said. "In my experience, this phase will move fast. Do you have a few more days of working the floor of the restaurant in you?"

"I've been hanging in there so far," she said. "Tomorrow is my day off since Mondays are the slowest."

"I'll still have to go in during the morning to clean up the desktop files and keep up my work of finding accounting software for Charley," he said. "He's the only one who accesses the computer as far as I know, so he has to be the one behind the crimes."

"I'm wondering just how much Phillip is pushing the buttons," she stated. "Charley might be a pawn based on what you saw this morning."

"Then he'll most likely get a chance to turn state's witness if he's willing to testify against the others and bring down the whole operation," he stated. "Not a bad haul for your first time out on a big assignment."

She nodded, thinking she wouldn't feel successful at all if she didn't get help for Zoey. Would she push Ree away? How could Ree approach the subject? A confrontation? She quickly dismissed the idea. Zoey could withdraw further. A handwritten note? That might work.

Thunder rumbled in the sky. The air was heavy with humidity. A storm brewed.

QUINT MARKED AS many suspect accounts as he could before sending his findings over to Grappell. He ran over the facts in his head. Charley was involved in moving money. Phillip, Bald Guy and Ruddy Complexion were involved, but it was unclear exactly what their roles were. The money seemed significant. Where were the guns? He wrote the high-level update to the boss, giving a whole lot of the credit for their findings to Ree. She deserved to have accolades in her jacket for her work on this case.

Rain pelted the tin roof of the cabin, the noise so

loud they wouldn't be able to talk over it if they tried. He glanced over at her and saw her scribbling away on a piece of paper. He had no doubt that she had a dozen or so good reasons to convince Zoey, if that was her real name, to go to Austin.

"Do you want to talk me through your arguments?" he offered. "I might be a good sounding board."

Ree glanced at the door and froze. "Did you hear that?"

"As a matter of fact, I did," he stated, glancing around the room to ensure there was nothing out in the open that could identify them as law enforcement. He nodded toward the door as he moved to his boot, strapping it on in record time.

"Who is it?" Ree shouted.

"Zoey." The young woman's voice shook. She had to be soaking, standing out in the rain.

Ree gave a quick look at Quint before opening the door. "You're drenched. Come on in."

Zoey stood there, still in her work clothes, with mascara-stained cheeks, looking about as pitiful as a soaked dog who'd escaped the backyard and gotten itself lost.

Zoey's gaze flew to Quint and then back at Ree. She shook her head but didn't budge. The momentary look of fear in her eyes would probably haunt Quint for weeks. Getting her help would be the only way to make it go away.

"It's okay," Ree soothed. She reached both hands out to Zoey, taking her arms and tugging her into the cabin. "Come in so we can close the door and get you out of this storm."

"It's just thunder scares me a little bit," Zoey said as she stood there dripping on the wood flooring.

Quint pushed up to standing and Zoey flinched. He had to force calm over himself because he knew exactly what that meant, and it caused a knot to form in his gut. "I'll just get a towel so she can dry off."

"Come sit down at the table," Ree continued, her voice tranquil as she led the young woman to a chair.

Quint retrieved a towel and brought it back. He walked the long way around whereas Zoey sat in the chair closest to the door. Smart strategy in case she decided to bolt. He handed Ree the towel and then retrieved three Cokes from the fridge. He held one up and Zoey gave a slight nod.

Again, after he opened the drink, he handed it over to Ree to give to Zoey.

"This place is too small for me to go in another room, but I can sit out in the car if the two of you need some privacy," he offered.

Zoey's eyes widened in surprise. She sat still for a long moment before giving a slight headshake.

"Okay, then, I'll just be over here watching a game." He motioned toward the laptop. On his way back to the couch, he snagged a pair of earbuds. He took a seat, tucked in the earbuds and pulled up a random game. He didn't turn on the volume because he wanted to hear the conversation as much as possible through the driving rain.

"My boyfriend and I had a fight," Zoey said quietly. "He kicked me out."

"Do you need a place to stay tonight?" Ree asked.

From the corner of his eye, he saw the young woman's lip quiver. She didn't respond.

"It's okay. You don't have to say. We can sit here and talk if you want. Or not. You can dry off, drink a Coke and chill." Ree set the Coke bottle in front of Zoey before picking up her own and taking a big swig.

Zoey started drying off as she picked up the Coke and took a sip. "Why do you care if I eat?"

"Because you need food," Ree replied casually.

"You shouldn't care," she said. "And I'm not a kid."

"You know what? I don't even like kids. We certainly don't have any and I don't know if I ever will. I have nephews who have so much energy they make me want to walk out of the room every time they zip past," Ree said with that same calm, collected voice.

Zoey rolled her eyes. "Kids, right?"

"They can be such a pain," Ree agreed. "So, as long as we establish that I'm not trying to be your mother, we're good."

Zoey nodded.

"I'd rather be friends anyway," Ree said. "Being new in town is hard on the social life."

"My boyfriend gets in these rages when I do something wrong and, like, takes everything. He's still angry at me for losing my key," she said.

"Losing a key isn't such a terrible thing," Ree said.

Strangely enough, it was probably Quint, rather than Ree, who could relate to Zoey's past. Ree came from a loving family and a solid home. Quint's background was a little more complicated. But at least he'd had his mother and Officer Jazz. Ree had been right earlier. Zoey had no one.

"Do you have family in Texas?" Ree asked.

"Nah, my mom ditched a couple of years ago. She didn't tell my stepdad before she took off. We weren't close to any other family. I'm probably the last person she wants to see again," she said like it was nothing, but there was an undercurrent of hurt in her voice. She was too relaxed when talking about the abandonment, showing too much of a forced, careless attitude.

Quint never crossed a line when it came to investigations because it might risk the operation. He'd learned to detach, focus on the good he was doing. But he couldn't allow this young woman to continue to be treated this way. This time, he had to put himself on the line.

Chapter Twenty

"Have you thought about other options?" Ree asked. She was making progress with Zoey but they were running out of time.

"What options?" Zoey fired back. "Take off by myself? I tried that once. Didn't work out. I'm nineteen. No one wants to rent to me."

"There are places—"

Zoey was already shaking her head. "Like shelters? No, thanks. I had a friend 'saved' by CPS once. She ended up in juvie after fighting off her foster dad."

Ree knew there were bad eggs in every system. People who viewed taking in fosters as money in the bank. Conditions could be harsh in an overburdened system. Those were the cases people talked about. Those were the cases that made headlines. She understood why, but there were so many success stories that didn't get the attention they deserved.

"I had a friend who got in trouble with a relationship. She didn't have family, either, so she found a place. It worked for her," Ree said, making up the story as she went along.

Zoey shot a curious look as she picked up her Coke and took another sip.

"I'm sure there are places that focus on young people," Ree said.

"Maybe," was all Zoey said.

Inch by inch, this was progress.

This was tough because Ree didn't have a whole lot of time to convince Zoey to get help. Come on too strong and Zoey would retreat.

"My friend went to this place in Austin after she got kicked out by her parents. It turned her life around. She got an associate degree and works in a community outreach program." Ree hated lying but she needed to create a composite so Zoey would have someone to relate to. Since her friend's experience in foster care caused her to shy away, Ree had to find a good counter.

"Really?" Zoey shrugged. "I don't know."

The fact she hadn't turned her nose up to the idea meant Ree had found the right approach.

"I could ask her where she went and give you the information if you think you might like to check it out," Ree offered. "Might be nice to be able to keep the money you work for. Save it to go to college or use it to buy a car."

The freedom idea seemed to strike another chord.

"I need a car, right?" Zoey's brown eyes widened. "Willie doesn't think so but I keep telling him that I can't even go to the grocery store by myself."

"Beats walking everywhere," Ree said. She

laughed, figuring it would help break up some of the tension. "But my car is only one step up."

"I know, right." Zoey winced, made a face, and then laughed.

"Hey, you were supposed to tell me it's not that bad," Ree quipped.

"But, like, have you seen it?" Zoey fired back. She had a wicked sense of humor. "I'm glad you stuck around."

"Thanks," Ree said. "Me, too."

Since time was running out, Ree decided she had to push a little on the shelter.

"Did you decide about whether or not you'd consider giving Austin a try?" Ree asked. She tried her level best not to give away just how much it meant to her.

"I mean, can't hurt. Right?" she hedged but there wasn't a whole lot of conviction in her voice.

All Ree could do was try.

"I'll reach out to my friend and bring the info to work with me tomorrow," Ree said, resisting the urge to oversell the idea. "So, how about tonight? Do you have a place to stay? We have a sofa bed that's available."

From the corner of her eye, she saw Quint look away from his screen and at her.

"Willie might get mad if I stay away all night," Zoey reasoned.

"You could text him," Ree offered. "Tell him you're with a friend from work."

Zoey folded her arms across her chest and sat a

little straighter. It was the moment that caused Ree to realize she'd pushed too far.

"I better head back," Zoey said. "The rain isn't so bad now."

"Do you want a ride?" Ree asked, figuring she needed to take a step back at this point. Plus, giving Zoey a ride had a double benefit. One, Zoey wouldn't be walking in the rain. Two, Ree would find out where Zoey lived.

"Yeah, sure. I guess," Zoey said. She drained her Coke before holding the empty bottle in the air. "There a trash can?"

"Just leave it on the table. I can take care of it later," Ree said like it was no big deal.

"You sure?" Zoey asked.

"Positive." Ree stood up. "Let's get you home."

Zoey stood.

"Leaving so soon?" Quint asked, pretending he hadn't been listening this whole time. He stood up and walked over to Ree, placing a soft hand on her arm before kissing her. "Where are the two of you off to?"

"Driving Zoey home," Ree said. "Do you want to come?"

"Sure, if it's okay with Zoey," he said.

Zoey blushed as she shrugged. She tried to play it off like it was no big deal but her actions said she had a crush on Quint. Seriously, though, who wouldn't?

QUINT GRABBED HIS cell from the table and then held the door for Zoey and Ree. His actions in the past couple of minutes were deliberate. He wanted to demonstrate a healthy relationship to the young woman if only for a few minutes while she was visiting. The little things had made a big impact on his life when he was a kid, especially when they came from someone he respected. It was clear to him Zoey looked up to Ree.

The car ride was short. Ree and Zoey chatted about the brunch crowd and working at Greenlight. As they pulled up to the address Zoey had provided, Ree asked, "How long have Fender and Adrian been together?"

"You noticed that, too?" Zoey asked.

"Hard to miss," Ree said, and he could tell she was hedging her bets.

"I know, right?" Zoey said, rolling her eyes. "They try to be so sneaky about it but it's so obvious."

Zoey was observant. Then again, it was probably a survival skill.

"I didn't catch on right away," Ree said.

"They've been on and off," Zoey admitted. "I think they've been on a break recently."

"Makes sense," Ree said. "Plus, I've been trying to get the lay of the land. Learning that place is like drinking from a fire hose."

Zoey laughed. "Yeah, I can see that."

"I'm getting the hang of it. I think," Ree continued.

"You? You've been great. You should have seen my first week," Zoey said, reaching for the handle. "Thanks for the ride."

"Do you know who Phillip is?" Ree asked.

Zoey's eye widened before she said, "All I know is that when he shows up, Charley gets nervous."

"I'll steer clear of him then," Ree said.

"Good idea," Zoey confirmed.

"Be careful," Ree warned.

"With Willie, I don't exactly have to do anything to get into trouble," she said as she exited the car.

"Be good to yourself," Ree said to Zoey.

The young woman smiled awkwardly but there was a genuine appreciation in her eyes.

"You, too," Zoey stated before shutting the door.

Both were silent until they made it a good distance from the small shack of a home Zoey shared with her boyfriend.

"It took everything inside me to hold back during my conversation with her," Ree admitted.

"You got her thinking. You said just the right amount," he defended.

"Did you see how fast she decided it was time to go when I pushed too far?" she asked.

"Yes. You pushed her buttons and she wasn't quite ready to face what that meant," he said. "Believe me, you did good."

"What will she do when the restaurant is shut down?" Ree asked on a sigh. "I can't seem to let that go. She'll be out of a job with no way to provide for herself. We're going to be hurting her even more."

"Hopefully it won't matter because by then, she'll be in Austin," he said.

Ree fisted her hands, placing them on top of her thighs.

"This is hard," she admitted. "I'm usually so clear on an assignment that I'm doing the right thing. It's obvious. There's a bad guy who is hurting others. I make sure said bad guy is locked away for as long as he deserves. The streets are safer. I sleep easy at night."

"I understand," he said. "This assignment is complicated. Some are."

"The last thing I want to do is hurt an innocent young woman," she said.

"Because you're in this for the right reasons," he reminded her. "This is hard. There are going to be casualties. Good people are going to have to figure out another move. I don't like that any more than you do. However, I will also submit that leaving the status quo can hurt folks even more."

"I'm listening," she said.

"Is Zoey's relationship with her boyfriend healthy?" he asked.

"Absolutely not."

"Is leaving Zoey in her present environment keeping her safe?" he continued.

"No. I don't believe it is."

"Could she end up more at risk if it was too easy to stay right where she is?" he asked.

Ree paused for a long moment.

"Yes," she finally said. "Leaving her in this environment could hurt her even more."

"Forcing a change breaks folks out of their comfort

zone," he said. "And that's when growth can happen. Leave her here and who knows what will happen the next time she breaks into someone's home for food."

Ree gasped.

"You're right," she said. "Zoey was lucky it was just the two of us. She could have gotten herself into real trouble."

"What if someone had been home?" he continued.

"Right again," she said before reaching over and touching his arm. "Thanks for talking me off the ledge."

"It's what we do for each other," he said.

"You say that like it's nothing but it means a lot to me," she said quietly. "I've always been in my brothers' shadows. They've always looked out for me but in a smothering way if that makes sense."

"I can see where that might happen," he agreed.

"You are nothing like them, by the way," she quickly added. "And despite my mistakes, I haven't doubted your trust in me."

"We all make mistakes, Ree."

"And beat ourselves up worse for them than anyone else ever could," she pointed out.

He thought about that for a long moment. She was right. He'd been torturing himself over what had happened to Tessa. Maybe it was time to learn how to move forward without her, without the shame, without the guilt.

"Thanks, Ree."

"For what?" she asked.

"Saying something that I needed to hear," he said.

Rather than speak, she leaned over the armrest and rested her head on his shoulder.

The rain was down to a drizzle. Parts of the roads were flooded. He navigated them back to the cabin, figuring it had been a day.

"Seems like the fight we heard last night between Adrian and Fender was nothing more than two lovers hashing it out," she said as he parked.

"Dating a coworker is always a bad idea," he stated. "I did it early in my career and regretted it every time."

Ree shifted to sitting straight up in her seat, breaking off all physical contact. He hadn't meant for that to happen even though it was probably for the best. Quint needed time to move on from his losses.

"Yeah, I can see where it would be a problem after a relationship ran its course," she said. There was a hint of sadness in her voice.

"Even the most promising ones fizzle out. Next thing you know, you're asking to be reassigned to avoid working with certain people," he continued. "It gets messy."

"Sounds awful," she agreed.

"It'll probably happen at some point in your career," he said. "Can't please everyone and this job does tend to attract strong personalities."

"That, I can see," was all she said as he parked in the spot in front of the cabin.

The minute he shut off the engine, she was out of the vehicle and through the front door. As awful as the hollowed-out feeling in his chest was, it would be best for both of them in the long run. This assignment would wrap very soon and the two of them would go their separate ways.

Quint was laying the groundwork for the inevitable.

Chapter Twenty-One

Ree ate, showered and crawled into bed without saying a word. She kept an earbud in and listened to some of her favorite tunes. "Middle of Nowhere" by Vancouver Sleep Clinic was her go-to song. But even that couldn't soothe her heart tonight.

By the next morning, Quint was back at the restaurant and she breathed a sigh of relief. Having him in the room and knowing this temporary situation was about to end sucked the air from her lungs.

She did her best to shake the feeling, reminding herself to breathe. She poured a cup of coffee and threw together enough of a breakfast to keep her from wanting to chew her arm off. The thought produced a melancholy smile. Hadn't she said the same thing to Quint not long after they'd met?

Grabbing her phone, she scrolled through their fake social media page. Bad idea. The two of them appeared so happy and in love. She had to admit, they were both good actors. If this law enforcement gig fell through, they could make money in Hollywood.

Ree scribbled down the name of the shelter in

Austin along with its website, tucked the piece of paper in her apron after she dressed for work.

Quint must have gotten sucked in by Charley because he still wasn't home by the time she headed out for work. Granted, she left fifteen minutes early so as not to spend any more time alone in a room with Quint than absolutely necessary. If she'd had a fantasy, even for five minutes, that something special was happening between the two of them he'd quashed any hope last night with a sledgehammer when he'd brought up the fact it was a bad idea to date a coworker.

No one had to tell Ree twice not to go where she wasn't welcome.

Zoey was already at work. There was no sign of Adrian. Ree figured this was a good time to hand over the note. She walked into Zoey's station. Out of the corner of her eye, she could swear she saw the guy from the bar, the one in the flannel shirt. Phillip.

"Hey," Ree said to Zoey's back.

The young woman jumped.

"Sorry." She turned around. There was no amount of makeup in the world that could cover those red, puffy eyes.

"Everything okay?" Ree asked, taking Zoey's hand and discreetly placing the folded-up slip of paper in it.

"Yeah. Sure. I always look like this when I don't sleep," Zoey said, brushing off the seriousness of what seemed to be happening at home.

"Take a look later." Ree nodded toward the paper in Zoey's hand.

The young woman quickly tucked it inside her apron. "I don't want to get yelled at for talking, so…"

"Of course not." Ree turned and walked back to her station, praying the teen didn't just toss the paper in the trash.

Adrian blew in at the last minute, looking frazzled and upset.

"Everything okay?" Ree asked as the woman breezed past.

"Is it ever?" Adrian asked before pushing open the kitchen door. "I need coffee."

"That's not an answer," Ree said, following. "Seriously, are you doing all right?"

"I won't be if I get my butt fired," Adrian said, grabbing a coffee cup. "This job is how I keep a roof over my head and pay my babysitter."

"You have a kid?" Ree asked, realizing how little she knew about Adrian.

"Yes, but please don't tell anyone about him," she whispered. "He's a year old."

Adrian pulled her cell phone from her apron and tapped the screen. "Here he is."

"What a cutie," Ree said and meant it. Was Fender the father?

"Thanks. He is my heart." Adrian practically beamed as she tucked her cell inside her apron and fixed a cup of coffee.

"Do you want me to put your stuff in your locker?" Ree asked.

"Would you?" Adrian asked, handing over her handbag.

"Go to the bathroom and fix your hair before Charley sees you," Ree whispered. Then she held up the bag. "Do you need anything from in here?"

Adrian grabbed a comb and a travel-size bottle of hairspray before rushing out of the room. Ree listened for the sound of keystrokes coming from the office. Click. Click. Clack.

She walked over and knocked on the door before sticking her head in.

"Missed you this morning," she said to Quint.

"Class was canceled, so I decided to stick around and see what I could get done today," he said before stretching out his arms. He pushed to standing, leaned over and kissed her. The minute their lips touched, a familiar jolt of electricity rocketed through Ree.

"I might just stick around for lunch at this point," he said, a little breathless from the kiss.

"I'll see you later, then," Ree said. She rushed to put up Adrian's bag and hurry back to the floor. The doors had already opened, and Zoey waited on the first table as two men walked inside the restaurant. Bald Guy and Ruddy Complexion. Ree's heart hammered her ribs from the inside out.

"Welcome to Greenlight," she said, forcing a smile. "Table for two?"

Bald Guy nodded. There was something decidedly creepy about this man. She'd arrested some dark individuals. There was something truly evil in the eyes of the most hardened criminals. Bald Guy fit into that category more so than Ruddy Complexion.

Ree led them to one of her tables in the middle of the room. She turned around to Bald Guy, who was shaking his head. He motioned toward the bar area.

"Sorry, it's closed," she said.

Bald Guy shot a murderous look at her. He motioned toward the bar area again.

Quint's stomach growled. He glanced at the clock. Lunch called. He powered down the computer, grabbed his coffee mug and headed to the dining room. He walked around to the counter and took a seat.

One look at Ree, and he knew something was up. She stood at a table talking to a couple, shifting her weight from left to right, and back. She nodded her head a little too enthusiastically. Something was off with her behavior.

He wished he could scan the dining room. This spot gave him a view to the kitchen.

Three cups of coffee kicked in and he had to use the bathroom. He opened the napkin in front of him and took out the knife and fork so someone would realize he was sitting there after setting his coffee cup down.

He took care of business and stood at the sink, washing his hands as the door opened. Bald Guy stepped inside, his gaze intent on Quint. His hand was inside his shirt.

Bald Guy pulled out a Glock, and then pointed the business end directly at Quint. There was a silencer on the end of it, which would keep the shot quiet. At this distance, Bald Guy couldn't miss. "You're a cop."

"No. What are going to do with all the blood?" Quint asked. "Have you thought about that? Because you should. This is a small room and I'm a bleeder."

The question seemed to catch Bald Guy off guard.

"Didn't consider that before you came in here and pulled that thing on me?" Quint goaded.

Bald Guy pulled a cloth bag out of his back pocket. He tossed it at Quint's chest.

"Put it over your head," the man said, his voice vaguely familiar.

"Where do I know you from?" Quint asked.

"Just do what I say," the man demanded.

This wasn't going well. If Quint recognized this person's voice, it was highly likely he'd been involved with another case. Did Bald Guy realize Quint was an agent?

This was bad. Quint took two seconds to evaluate his options. He could possibly fire off a kick in time to knock the weapon out of Bald Guy's hand. But his finger hovered over the trigger as it was, and he could pull it by accident. Of course, he could pull the trigger on purpose and that wouldn't bode well for Quint, either, at this range. The distance between where Quint stood and the door was too far for Quint to make a move.

Just when he was about to place the bag over his head, the door opened, slamming into Bald Guy's back. He threw an elbow to stop the person on the other side from opening the door all the way. But the moment of distraction gave Quint the window he needed. He fired off a roundhouse kick, connecting with Bald Guy's hand, which was knocked hard to the right. The weapon fired soon after Quint's left heel connected. The cold metal slammed against the opposite wall.

A momentary look of panic washed over Bald Guy's face, but he recovered. He lunged toward Quint. This guy had the size and speed of a linebacker going after a quarterback. Quint used it against the guy. As Bald Guy dove toward Quint, he grabbed two fistfuls of Bald Guy's shirt, dropped down on his back, and helped momentum toss Bald Guy into the wall, headfirst.

There was a concussion waiting to happen as Bald Guy's head snapped to one side and his neck took most of the impact. At the same time, the door opened.

"Quint," Ree said, rushing inside and closing the door behind her. She pulled out her cell and immediately called the situation in.

Bald Guy lay crumpled on the tile floor as Quint located the man's Glock and immediately emptied it. Quint patted the guy down to see if he had any other weapons. He didn't. Quint tucked the empty gun in the back of his waistband as he ushered Ree out the door.

Charley was running down the hallway toward them. "What happened?"

Chapter Twenty-Two

"A guy pulled out a gun and tried to shoot me while I was going to the bathroom," Quint said, making it seem like he was trying to catch his breath. "It's your 'associate' from the other morning."

Charley's eyes widened.

"I'm sorry. This is a business deal that's gone bad. I'll take care of it," he promised, waving his arms in the air.

"Take care of it?" Ree asked. She had one question. Was it possible their cover wasn't blown? "I called the sheriff. This guy needs to be arrested. He's dangerous and just tried to shoot my husband for no reason."

She turned her mouth sideways to Quint when she whispered, "He came in with Ruddy Complexion."

"I can handle this, Ree," Charley warned. "Get back in the kitchen."

Those words sliced through Ree with the efficiency of a blade. She stalked toward Charley. As soon as she came within reach, she poked her index finger in his chest.

"Don't you dare ever tell me to, 'get back in the kitchen' again," she practically growled.

"Stop," came the small voice. Zoey's voice.

She came around the corner.

"All this noise and yelling has run off all our customers," she said, her cheeks red with anger.

In the next moment, Ruddy Complexion grabbed her and started dragging her backward toward the front door. She screamed and flailed.

Ree stood there, helpless, flinching at the gun pointed at Zoey's temple.

"No, Willie," she screamed.

"Stop," Ree said.

"I told you not to look at me or say my real name in public," Willie admonished. "And I'll slit your throat before I go back to jail."

"Stop," Ree commanded in unison with Quint.

Charley took a step to the side, looking bewildered and like he couldn't begin to process things as they were happening so fast.

Quint bolted out the side door, setting off the fire alarm. Ree ran toward Zoey, realizing that she needed to create a diversion if Quint was going to succeed in surprising Willie.

QUINT KNEW EXACTLY where Willie was headed, the SUV. So Quint kept a low profile and beat Willie to it. Zoey was struggling, which was a distraction. Ultimately, Quint didn't believe Willie would physically hurt Zoey but he seemed to have no qualms about using her to get away.

But get away where?

The guy's days were numbered because his identity was now known. Then again, if he was involved with the money laundering scheme, he could be connected to a bigger organization that would send him underground for a while until everything cooled off.

Quint could not let Willie, aka Ruddy Complexion, get away with Zoey. Period.

Sirens sounded in the distance. The cavalry was on its way. And yet, if Willie got Zoey in that vehicle, there would be little to celebrate. Quint couldn't allow that to happen. He kept a low profile behind the SUV as Willie forced Zoey around to the driver's side.

"Don't do this, Willie," Ree demanded. Good, she was keeping Willie's attention on her. It would give Quint the element of surprise he needed.

Wait a few more seconds. Let Willie get a little closer.

Willie moved to the back seat, opened the door and started to stuff Zoey inside. Quint made his move. He dove toward the man, tackling him at his knees. Quint heard a snap, and seriously hoped the broken bone was on Willie's body and not Quint's.

He took a hard elbow to the back of the neck as he wrestled Willie to the ground. The glint of metal being raised in the air sent a jolt of adrenaline rocketing through Quint. All he could think was *hell, no*.

Quint spun like an alligator with prey in its jaws. Willie grunted as his extended hand met the gravel pavement. He managed to keep his fingers clasped around the weapon but he took some damage with the move.

Before Willie could get his bearings, Quint pressed his powerful thighs around the man's midsection, squeezing the air from his lungs.

Willie coughed and grunted, trying to shift the balance of power by gouging Quint in the back with his free hand. Quint squeezed harder. He threw a punch that landed with a head snap, and then went for the knife.

It was a mistake to be too eager. Willie managed to free his arm, and jabbed the knife toward Quint's midsection. Quint shifted his weight in time to miss the blade, catching Willie by the wrist.

Squeezing his thighs with every ounce of strength he had left, he wrestled the knife out of Willie's hand as the sheriff's SUV came roaring up. Willie's face was beet red. He made one final attempt to punch Quint, who caught Willie's other wrist and pushed his hands up over his head, easing up on the pressure to the man's midsection.

"Hands high where I can see 'em," the sheriff said.

"No can do, sir," Quint replied. "This man is a danger. You can come take him from me, but I will not release my grip until I know it's safe to do so."

The sheriff didn't lower his weapon as he moved toward the pair of men. He got close enough to cuff Willie despite the fact he struggled the entire time.

"You got him?" Quint asked the sheriff.

"That's affirmative," came the response.

Quint rolled over and let the sheriff take over. He forced Willie to his feet as Quint heaved for air. The back-to-back fights had left him winded. Ree came over to him, and dropped down beside him.

"There's a man in the restroom who tried to shoot me," Quint informed the sheriff. "He probably needs an ambulance."

Charley's cousin secured Willie in the back of his vehicle. Next, he radioed for an ambulance before disappearing into the building.

Zoey sat on the bench seat of the SUV, looking lost and alone. Quint caught Ree's attention. "You can go to her."

"But you're hurt," she said. "I don't want to leave you."

Quint tried to scoot over to lean his back on the SUV. Two of the fingers on his right hand were jacked up at odd angles. His pointer and middle finger would be getting real close to each other in the coming weeks. And he planned to take some time off work after this case.

"Go on. I'm not going anywhere," he assured her.

Ree went to Zoey, who crumpled into Ree's arms. Ree glanced over at Quint as she patted Zoey's back and held her.

He made the call to let his boss know what had gone down. She in turn made the call to the sheriff personally. Ten minutes later, Charley came outside in handcuffs as a deputy arrived.

This operation was busted.

"LOOKS LIKE IT'S moving day," Quint said to Ree as he loaded the last of his suitcases with his good hand.

"Are you sure you don't want to go to the ER to have that thing checked out properly?" she asked.

He lifted his right hand.

"What? This? The EMTs did a bang-up job," he said with a smile.

"Even he said you should go to the hospital," she countered.

"Don't worry about it," he said. "I have a guy back home. He'll fix me right up."

Ree moved to the fridge and opened a Coke.

"Is it weird that I'm sad to leave? We've only been here a few days," she said. "Why do I feel an attachment to this place?"

"I don't know. Cricket Creek has its good side," he offered.

A piece of him wished he was the reason, but that was just silly. They had separate lives to go back to, and despite the feeling they'd become closer than two people should who weren't wearing matching rings, they barely knew each other.

"Zoey agreed to go to Austin," Ree said. "She's on a bus now."

"That's good," he said.

"I'm thinking about doing a little research when I get home," she said.

"What kind?" he asked.

"Puppy adoption," she said. "It's probably crazy. Right?"

"I've heard of worse things," he said. "Just give yourself a day or two before you make any decisions."

"Heat of the moment?"

"It could be," he said. "Somehow, I doubt it with you but a decision as big as that one should breathe for a few days before you make any commitments."

She nodded.

"I thought I'd take it to Zoey when she got her own place. I'd like to stay in touch with her at the very least," she said.

"Good for you, and her," he said. "Having a mentor turned my life around."

"Your story gave me the inspiration," she admitted and his heart took a hit.

His cell buzzed as he closed up the suitcase. He fished it out and checked the screen.

"Grappell," he said to her before answering. "I'm putting you on speaker."

"Hi, Ree," Grappell said.

"Hey, yourself," Ree called out.

"I'm sure you'll have your wrap-up interviews soon but I thought you might want to know what I found out about the case," Grappell said.

"Fire away," Quint said.

"Turns out that Charley is already rolling over. Phillip Mancuso was the one forcing Charley to run weapons through the restaurant but he's been teeing up for greater things at Greenlight. He was getting pushback from Charley."

Quint perked up. "Any chance this guy is—"

"He is. I thought you'd want to know the name that came up and where this investigation is headed once things cool off," Grappell said.

"Can't be," Quint said as Ree's forehead creased with confusion.

"The name that is coming up as being linked in all this is Dumitru," Grappell supplied. "Phillip has ties to A-12."

Hearing that name sucked all the air out of the room. Quint's lips compressed into a frown.

"Is he…?" Ree seemed to catch on.

"Get me on the assignment when this thing happens," Quint demanded.

"It'll never happen," Grappell said. "We both know it."

"Nothing is set in stone," Quint stated. He needed to be the one to investigate the man who caused his best friend to die.

"This will be," Grappell said. "I just thought you should know."

Quint thanked him before ending the call. His mind was already working, figuring a way to get himself on the assignment.

"Can I give you a ride home?" Ree asked as she closed up her suitcase. She finished her Coke and then tossed the empty bottle in the trash.

"I have the motorcycle," he said.

"You can have it towed," she stated. "You can't ride like that." She motioned toward his hand. "Besides, you have a suitcase."

"I can strap it on the back of my motorcycle like I did on the way here," he said. "Plus, the open air will clear my head."

Ree picked up her suitcase and walked to the door.

She stopped, set it down and turned around. Her green eyes sparkled with a mix of need and determination as she made a beeline toward him and into his arms. Against all better judgment, he dipped his head down and claimed those full lips of hers one more time. She parted her lips enough to give him better access before teasing his tongue inside her mouth. Quint's heart fisted as need welled inside him with the force of a rogue wave, intense and all-consuming. He brought his hands up to cup her face as she dug her fingernails into his shoulders. Their breathing quickened and an ache formed in his chest. The need to feel her skin-to-skin crashed into him.

A reminder she wasn't his to explore nailed his gut. He pulled back midkiss before his heart passed the point of no return, and leaned his forehead against hers for a long moment. Trying to slow his pulse to something within reasonably normal range took all the energy he had left.

"I know you're going after him," she finally said before pressing those sweet lips of hers against his one more time. "Watch out for your blind spots."

Walking away from a successful assignment had never hollowed out his chest before. He did his level best to ignore the pain but the ache was taking hold.

"Give me a call if you ever want to go out for a beer sometime," she said, lingering at the door. Her tongue slicked across her bottom lip, leaving a silky trail—a trail he wanted to spend more time exploring.

"I plan to take you up on that." Quint took in a

sharp breath and smiled, needing for her to leave before he changed his mind, got all soft and asked her to stick around.

She stood there for a long moment, staring down at her bag. Then she lifted her head up, bit down on her bottom lip and walked away.

* * * * *

USA TODAY *bestselling author Barb Han's series,* A Ree and Quint Novel, *continues next month with*

Newlywed Assignment.

You'll find it wherever *Harlequin Intrigue books are sold!*

COMING NEXT MONTH FROM

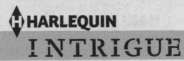

#2073 STICKING TO HER GUNS
A Colt Brothers Investigation • by B.J. Daniels

Tommy Colt is stunned when his childhood best friend—and love—
Bella Worthington abruptly announces she's engaged to their old-time nemesis!
Knowing her better than anyone, Tommy's convinced something is dangerously
wrong. Now Colt Brothers Investigations' newest partner is racing to uncover the
truth and ask Bella a certain question...if they survive.

#2074 FOOTHILLS FIELD SEARCH
K-9s on Patrol • by Maggie Wells

When two kids are kidnapped from plain sight, Officer Brady Nichols and his
intrepid canine, Winnie, spring into action. Single mother Cassie Whitaker thought
she'd left big-city peril behind—until it followed her to Jasper. But can Brady and
his K-9 protect Cassie from a stalker who won't take no for an answer?

#2075 NEWLYWED ASSIGNMENT
A Ree and Quint Novel • by Barb Han

Hardheaded ATF legend Quint Casey knows he's playing with fire asking
Agent Ree Sheppard to re-up as his undercover wife. To crack a ruthless Houston
weapons ring, they must keep the mission—and their explosive chemistry—under
control. But Quint's determined need for revenge and Ree's risky moves are
putting everything on the line...

#2076 UNDERCOVER RESCUE
A North Star Novel Series • by Nicole Helm

After the husband she thought was dead returns with revenge on his mind,
Veronica Shay resolves to confront her secret past—and her old boss,
Granger Macmillan, won't let her handle it on her own. But when they fall into a
nefarious trap, they'll call in their entire North Star family in order to stay alive...

#2077 COLD CASE CAPTIVE
The Saving Kelby Creek Series • by Tyler Anne Snell

Returning to Kelby Creek only intensifies Detective Lily Howard's guilt at the
choice she made years ago to rescue her childhood crush, Anthony Perez, rather
than pursue the man abducting his sister. But another teen girl's disappearance
offers a chance to work with Ant again—and a tantalizing new lead that could
mean inescapable danger.

#2078 THE HEART-SHAPED MURDERS
A West Coast Crime Story • by Denise N. Wheatley

Attacked and left with a partial heart-shaped symbol carved into her chest,
forensic investigator Lena Love finds leaving LA to return to her hometown comes
with its own danger—like detective David Hudson, the love she left behind.
But soon bodies—all marked with the killer's signature heart—are discovered in
David's jurisdiction...

*Wedding bells and shotgun fire are ringing out
in Lonesome, Montana. Read on for another
Colt Brothers Investigation novel from* New York Times
bestselling author B.J. Daniels.

Bella Worthington took a breath and, opening her eyes, finally faced her reflection in the full-length mirror. The wedding dress fit perfectly—just as he'd said it would. While accentuating her curves, the neckline was modest, the drape flattering. As much as she hated to admit it, Fitz had good taste.

The sapphire-and-diamond necklace he'd given her last night gleamed at her throat, bringing out the blue-green of her eyes—also like he'd said it would. He'd thought of everything—right down to the huge pear-shaped diamond engagement ring on her finger. All of it would be sold off before the ink dried on the marriage license—if she let it go that far.

As she studied her reflection, though, she realized this was exactly as he'd planned it. She looked the beautiful bride on her wedding day. No one would be the wiser.

She could hear music and the murmur of voices downstairs. He'd invited the whole town of Lonesome, Montana. She'd watched from the upstairs window as the guests had arrived earlier. He'd wanted an audience for this and now he would have one.

The knock at the door startled her, even though she'd been expecting it. "It's time," said a male voice on the other side. One of Fitz's hired bodyguards, Ronan, was waiting. He would be carrying a weapon under his suit. Security, she'd been told, to keep her safe. A lie.

She listened as Ronan unlocked her door and waited outside, his boss not taking any chances. He had made sure there was no possibility of escape short of shackling her to her bed. Fitz was determined that she find no way out of this. It didn't appear that she had.

In a few moments, she would be escorted downstairs to where her maid of honor and bridesmaids were waiting—all handpicked by her groom. If they'd questioned why they were down there and she was up here, they hadn't asked. He wasn't the kind of man women questioned. At least not more than once.

For another moment, Bella stared at the stranger in the mirror. She didn't have to wonder how she'd gotten to this point in her life. Unfortunately, she knew too well. She'd just never thought Fitz would go this far. Her mistake. He, however, had no idea how far she was willing to go to make sure the wedding never happened.

Taking a breath, she picked up her bouquet from her favorite local flower shop. The bouquet had been a special order delivered earlier. Her hand barely trembled as she lifted the blossoms to her nose for a moment, taking in the sweet scent of the tiny white roses—also his choice. Carefully, she separated the tiny buds, afraid it wouldn't be there.

It took her a few moments to find the long, slim silver blade hidden among the roses and stems. The blade was sharp, and lethal if used correctly. She knew exactly how to use it. She slid it back into the bouquet out of sight. He wouldn't think to check it. She hoped. He'd anticipated her every move and attacked with one of his own. Did she really think he wouldn't be ready for anything?

Making sure the door was still closed, she checked her garter. What she'd tucked under it was still there, safe, at least for the moment.

Another knock at the door. Fitz would be getting impatient and no one wanted that. "Everyone's waiting," Ronan said, tension in his tone. If this didn't go as meticulously planned, there would be hell to pay from his boss. Something else they all knew.

She stepped to the door and opened it, lifting her chin and straightening her spine. Ronan's eyes swept over her with a lusty gaze, but he stepped back as if not all that sure of her. Clearly he'd been warned to be wary of her. Probably just as she'd been warned what would happen if she refused to come down—or worse, made a scene in front of the guests.

At the bottom of the stairs, the room opened and she saw Fitz waiting for her with the person he'd hired to officiate.

He was so confident that he'd backed her into a corner with no way out. He'd always underestimated her. Today would be no different. But he didn't know her as well as he thought. He'd held her prisoner, threatened her, forced her into this dress and this ruse.

But that didn't mean she was going to marry him.

She would kill him first.

HIEXP0322INC

Get 4 FREE REWARDS!

We'll send you 2 FREE Books plus 2 FREE Mystery Gifts.

FREE Value Over $20

Both the **Harlequin Intrigue®** and **Harlequin® Romantic Suspense** series feature compelling novels filled with heart-racing action-packed romance that will keep you on the edge of your seat.

Lena Love kicked a rock out from underneath her foot, then
bent down and tightened the twill shoelaces on her brown
leather hiking boots.

The crime scene investigator, who doubled as a forensic
science technician, stood back up and eyed Los Angeles's
Cucamonga Wilderness trail. Sharp-edged stones and ragged
shards of bark covered the rugged, winding terrain.

"Watch your step," she uttered to herself before continuing
along the path of her latest crime scene.

Lena squinted as she focused on the trail. Heavy foliage
loomed overhead, blocking out the sun's brilliant rays. She
pulled out her flashlight, hoping its bright beam would help
uncover potential evidence.

An ominous wave of vulnerability swept through her
chest at the sight of the vast San Gabriel Mountains. She spun
around slowly, feeling small while eyeing the infinite views
of the forest, desert and snowy mountainous peaks.

The wild surroundings left her with a lingering sense of
defenselessness. Lena tightened the belt on her tan suede
blazer. She hoped it would give her some semblance of
security.